THE PERFECT CHRISTMAS

THE PERFECT REGENCY SERIES, BOOK 3

ANNABELLE ANDERS

ANNABELLE
ANDERS

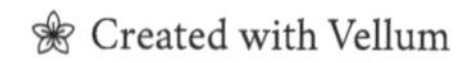
Created with Vellum

CONTENT NOTE

Bonus Material Added
By Annabelle Anders

Original version first published in
Yuletide Happily Ever After II
An Original Regency Romance Collection
For the 2019 Christmas Season

DEDICATION

This is a story about forgiveness. Over the course of a lifetime, a person is faced with millions of choices, some more difficult than others. And sometimes, we make the wrong ones.

In a world filled with hard consequences, all of us need grace.

And so I'm dedicating this book to those who practice grace.

PROLOGUE

ENGLAND, EARLY 1800'S

"Eliza, Mother asked me to remind you to wear your cap. She's displeased that you've left it off."

Matthew's voice carried that disapproving tone Eliza was beginning to resent. They were to be married in three weeks' time and she hoped this feeling was only temporary. Her actual duties at the Dog and Pudding Pot Inn did not bother her, but her future mother-in-law's constant nagging had not been something she'd bargained for. Her future in-laws were aging, however, and the plan was for Matthew and Eliza to eventually take ownership and run it as their own.

The stress of additional responsibilities had also taken their toll on Matthew. The two of them rarely had time to enjoy one another anymore.

Taking a deep breath, Eliza smoothed the counterpane on the bed before turning around to address him. "I only take it off because it itches. I'm not used to it, you know that. I'll wear it if I go into the public areas, but surely it isn't necessary while I'm cleaning the guest's room. No one ever sees me."

The man she'd considered to be so very handsome last summer scowled. Suddenly she was more aware that the blondish hair she'd compared to sunshine just months ago appeared to be thinning on top and his blue-grey eyes seemed a tad close together. Silly things that didn't really matter because she loved him, and they were to marry. It was just a phase. She was simply experiencing an unfortunate bout of cold feet.

She should not be so picky. He was a gentle soul, she reminded herself, dismissing her irritation. It was part of what had attracted her to him to begin with. Perhaps she could wear the dratted cap. If that would make things easier--

"Why must you be so obstinate? It's a small thing, and it would mean so much to Mother."

Eliza swallowed hard and then walked around the bed and proceeded to fluff the pillow — exerting perhaps slightly more vigor than necessary.

"Only until after the wedding," Matthew had crept up behind her, placing his hands upon her shoulders, his mouth near her ear.

She leaned back to take comfort from him. They'd been allowed so little time alone as of late. "Your mother hasn't mentioned their move lately. Do you think they'll be happy, living an idle life, away from the inn?" Mr. and Mrs. Wilson were planning to move south to live near Matthew's mother's sister after Matthew and Eliza were married and settled in.

Her betrothed released her and stepped away. When Eliza stared up at him, he didn't meet her eyes. "In due time. It's a big change."

"How much time, Matthew?" Eliza dropped the pillow and hugged her arms in front of herself.

"They might stay on a little longer, give us more time to learn the business. Mother says she feels revitalized to have us both helping out now. And Father says what with the money they save by not paying us a wage, we can add another wing to the back of the inn. If we had more rooms, the inn could easily support all of us."

Eliza blinked. Surely, he wasn't suggesting that they would all live together after their wedding.

Matthew smiled sweetly at her. "Please don't worry over these type of details. You trust me, don't you?" He tilted his head.

Of course, she trusted him! She loved him!

It would be all right. Everything was going to be fine. It was just that the role Matthew's parents expected of her wasn't one she'd planned on stepping into. She would do her best for now, to please them, but after the wedding…

She smiled up at her future husband. "You know that I do. And I'll try to remember the cap in the future."

She tilted her head back for the kiss she expected for some reassurance was disappointed when Matthew took a step backward instead. "Not in one of the guest rooms, Eliza." He grimaced.

She nodded, hating that she'd not considered that it might be inappropriate.

"Eliza?"

She smiled. He loved her. He'd not show her physical affection right now, but he'd reassure her with his words.

"Yes, Matthew?"

"Don't forget that cook needs your assistance after supper this evening. And put your cap on before mother sees you again." And with that reminder, he closed the door behind him, leaving her alone to finish preparing the room.

Eliza's own parents had allowed her considerable liberty while growing up, despite the fact that her father had been a vicar. She'd had a pleasant upbringing, really. Finances had only become tight after her father stepped down from his position. His thoughts had become muddled and after forgetting most of his sermon on one occasion, he'd felt it best for his parish that they bring in somebody new.

Eliza had only begun to feel pressure to marry when she realized her father's income had been cut by half. Her upkeep had become a burden.

She'd come to visit her brother, Thomas, last summer with the idea that she could assist him with his own parish for a few months. It would ease her parents' burden and give her time to contemplate her future. Although she was barely eight and ten, she'd been well educated and thought that rather than marrying, she might apply for a post as a governess, perhaps, or a teacher.

All of that had changed however, when she'd caught Matthew Wilson's attention. He was brawny, handsome and the son of successful merchants. She felt they suited one another rather well. He'd been considerate and charming and was all she'd imagined in a husband. Thomas, had approved of the match and she'd eagerly accepted her handsome suitor had dropped onto one knee and proposed.

When she'd promised herself to Matthew, however, she'd not expected that she'd be entering service. It was only after they'd announced their engagement that his parents suggested they take up the management of the inn, when her life had taken this turn.

Working as a maid, beneath his mother, was supposed to be temporary, though.

Something like fear squeezed her heart. Her wedding date was less than three weeks away. Her parents had been thrilled to no longer have to worry for her future. She'd not be a burden to her parents or her brother any longer. The engagement had been celebrated by all, including herself.

She'd imagined a small cottage and a few children. She'd imagined planting a garden with vegetables but also flowers.

She loved Matthew.

Eliza pressed a clenched fist against her mouth and turned back to stare at the bed she'd just made up.

Invitations had been sent. Family members from miles away planned on traveling great distances to attend. Her mother had told everyone she knew.

"Pardon me, Miss. I was told the room had already been readied."

Eliza dropped her hand from her mouth and spun around. A gentleman stood in the open door, a valise in one hand, his top hat in the other. He was tall, his head nearly reaching the top of the door frame. And he was slim, in an elegant way.

This particular man would never have to worry about thinning hair. Although he must be close to the age of thirty, his hair was thick and black and longer than was strictly fashionable. And his eyes, a deep green, the color of leaves in the forest just after a rain.

Struck by his… everything, Eliza stared at him in fascination.

"Perhaps I am in the wrong room? Number seven?" He smiled hesitantly.

"Yes." She shook herself out of the momentary trance she'd fallen into. "No. I mean, this is number seven. I'm almost finished." She rushed around the bed to gather her supplies, forcing her eyes to sweep the room for anything she might have forgotten.

"I believe I'm rather taken with this village. Have you lived in Misty Brooke long?" He'd set his valise on the floor and had walked over to stare out the window.

"Not until recently actually. I've lived most of my life in Blackhaven—a day's drive south of here. Blackhaven is so small that you miss it if you blink while passing through. But my brother has lived here for several years now. He's the local vicar and I've visited him often." She realized she was babbling but for the life of her couldn't stop herself.

He turned his gaze back inside and after studying her face for a moment, allowed it to slide down her person and then back up again.

She ought to feel insulted. She ought to frown in disapproval. She did neither.

"Blackhaven's loss is Misty Brooke's gain."

All the air, it seemed, had suddenly been sucked out of her lungs. Heat flushed through her veins and a roaring filled her ears as her stare clashed with his. There was nothing inappropriate in his comment, but the tone of his voice had been... low, sensual.

Approving.

When she could stand it no longer, she dropped her lashes. "Th--thank you." She managed. And then looked up again.

"Henry Fairchild." He bowed in her direction. "And you are?"

Eliza swallowed hard. "I am Miss Eliza Cline."

His eyes flared for a moment. "Miss Cline, I am delighted to make your acquaintance."

Eliza dipped into a curtsey. "Likewise, Mr. Fairchild." Suddenly she was all too aware that she wore a dingy looking apron over a plain brown, poor excuse of a dress.

And yet, he seemed to appreciate her appearance.

"Will you be staying in Misty Brooke long, Sir?" Standing behind the bed, as she was, she couldn't exit the room until he stepped out of her path.

He averted his gaze for a moment and twisted his mouth into a wince, but perhaps she'd imagined it, as he was all smiles when he turned back to answer. "I believe I just might."

Butterflies took flight inside her.

Most inappropriate butterflies.

Eliza berated them and willed them to settle down. She was an engaged woman and it was foolish to allow herself to be so utterly discomposed by a handsome face.

She straightened her back. "I hope you enjoy your stay, sir. If you'll excuse me." She went to pass through the narrow space between him and the bed, expecting he'd move away to give her more room.

But he did not.

As her body brushed his, those butterflies turned into shooting stars and every inch where she'd made contact with him sizzled with *something* startling. And that something startling was also *very inappropriate.*

"Good day, Miss Cline," his voice taunted her as she escaped through the door.

* * *

ELIZA TUGGED the uncomfortable cap off and tilted her head back to study the night sky. So many stars, twinkling, winking down at her. She closed her eyes and allowed the cool night breeze to cool her neck and cheeks.

She'd washed more dishes tonight, most likely, than she had over the course of her entire life.

Although murmurs rose and fell from laughter and sometimes a not–so–heated argument inside the tap room, outside it was quiet and peaceful. If she was at her father's house, she would venture into the woods but Matthew had instructed her not to go wandering alone.

And he was right, of course.

Even so, Eliza gazed longingly into the shadows.

"*Aschenputtel* is allowed a time of rest." The voice emerged from the darkness before the person did. *His* voice.

Tonight, he was not wearing his tightly fitted coat, nor a cravat. He wore elegant trousers, however, with an embroidered waistcoat and a pristine linen shirt.

Her eyes examined the lace at his wrists and then trailed up to his face.

Her heart jumped when their eyes met.

The very air that surrounded her seemed to change with his presence. It grew heavy, charged, as though lightning was not far off.

She smiled at him, recognizing his reference to the fairy tale immediately. "*Aschenputtel* gives me nightmares. I prefer the French version myself. Those Brother's Grimm are too dark for my liking."

He gestured toward the empty space on the bench. "May I?" At her nod he lowered himself beside her. "*Cendrillon* then? Practically a nursery rhyme. The story only becomes interesting when the evil stepsisters begin cutting off parts of their feet."

"And the birds peck out their eyes." She laughed. "I do admit to finding some satisfaction in their fate."

He'd turned so that he partially faced her. Only a few inches separated the two of them, reminding her of the reaction she'd had to him that afternoon. But they were only conversing. She was quite safe.

And yet, she mustn't allow herself to give the appearance of flirting with him, despite an almost irresistible urge to do so.

"I trust your meal was pleasant?" She attempted to erect the barriers of their different stations.

He didn't answer right away. It seemed he preferred to simply stare at her.

"What?" She reached up to brush at her cheek. "Have I something on my face?"

He shook his head. "I'm merely drinking in your beauty." He smiled so wide that she knew he was well aware of how ridiculous his compliment sounded. But then he grew serious, and his eyes, even more intense. "You may try to hide your loveliness, but I see it. I have not been fooled by your aprons and caps."

"Perhaps you can remind my fiancé of this." The words

escaped unchecked. Such a comment did not show Matthew in a good light. She sounded petty and self-pitying. She dropped her gaze to her lap. "Please, forget that I said that. I must be more tired than I thought."

What was wrong with her?

"The young Mr. Wilson? He's blind if he doesn't see what he has."

"How do you know who my fiancé is?" His comment had surprised her. He'd only just checked in and she and Matthew's engagement wasn't something anyone would have discussed with a guest.

"When I see a pretty girl, I like to know something about her." He raised a hand to his chest. "A dagger pierced me through and through when I discovered you were promised to another. I'll have you know, I found the news quite disagreeable, indeed."

How foolish.

Eliza frowned, still wondering who had been discussing such personal information about her with a perfect stranger.

"Mrs. Wilson, if you must know. It was your future mother-in-law who divulged the dreadful state of your affairs." Mr. Fairchild's voice sounded almost lazy, in his casual disapproval of Matthew's mother. "Mother-in-law. An altogether disagreeable pairing of words. Nothing wrong with a mother. They are perfectly wonderful beings. But add legal implications and..." He pretended to shudder and then grinned over at her.

Eliza couldn't help but laugh.

Oh, but she shouldn't. She truly should not!

"Your future mother-in-law did, however, inform me that if I needed anything at all, I was to bring my request to you."

"Did you have need of something then, Mr. Fairchild?" Eliza straightened her back and went to stand up. Whatever it was that he needed, she'd fetch it for him and then sneak away to her own small chamber to retire for the evening.

"Not at all. Quite the contrary." He placed a hand upon her leg, halting her from rising.

And then... he didn't remove it as he ought. Eliza dropped her lashes and studied that hand. Elegant, lean fingers, but they were not effeminate. They showed that he'd labored some.

It was, she thought in surprise, the most attractive hand she'd ever laid eyes upon.

His voice brought her attention back to his face. "I merely wished for some company, some pleasant conversation," he amended.

He could easily find conversation in the taproom. But...

How long had it been since she'd had an edifying conversation with anyone? Since she'd been able to discuss literature, or science, or art?

She smiled in some relief. "But let's not discuss the Brother's Grimm. I don't relish any nightmares tonight."

He lifted his hand off her leg and held it out to her. "Nothing to inspire nightmares. You will keep me company for a while? Do we have a deal then?"

What was she doing? She barely knew this man.

She allowed his hand to clasp hers firmly. "It's a deal, Mr. Fairchild."

He squeezed gently. "Henry." The depths of his eyes seemed almost unfathomable. "Please, call me Henry."

* * *

THREE NIGHTS LATER, and Eliza sat eagerly anticipating his arrival. Each night upon completing her tasks, she'd sat outside quite innocently until Henry came around for a late-night chat. He'd not promised her that he would come, and she'd not promised him that she would be here, but he had not checked out of the inn yet. He would tell her when he would leave. They had become friends.

She'd learned that he'd just traveled from London. He was the second son of a Baron and was slowly making his way home. He'd not been surprised, he said, to learn that she was the daughter of a vicar. She had an angelic glow.

She'd laughed at that.

Aside from a few flirtatious exchanges, their meetings were harmless.

She persistently reminded herself of this. He wouldn't be staying much longer, she'd reasoned. And afterward, they'd likely never see one another again.

Each night she'd invited Matthew to come outside to sit with her and he'd always refused. He was tired, he told her. But when she slipped back inside to go to her own chamber the night before, she'd caught a glimpse of him sitting in the tap room, conversing with some of their lodgers and drinking a mug of ale.

It was good for him to mingle with the guests. They would appreciate being entertained by the owner's son.

"No fairy godmother has rescued you yet?" He persisted in appearing out of the darkness, almost as though he'd been lying in wait for her. She dismissed the thought as foolishness. "*Aschenputtel* must toil another day."

Eliza scooted to her edge of the bench. "*Cendrillon*," she corrected him.

He did not drop down beside her tonight, however, as he had on the previous evenings. Instead he extended a hand. "Come walk with me tonight."

She'd felt safe sitting on the bench, sitting outside the back of the inn's kitchen. Not that she feared Henry in any way, but she feared being seen by any gossips. Walking alone with him would have an appearance of impropriety.

She stared at his hand but only paused for a moment.

Ignoring the small voice of warning in the back of her mind, she reached out and allowed him to clasp her hand in his. It did not feel improper, or dangerous when she walked beside him. He was her friend. He was older and wiser and stronger. How could anything bad happen if he was there to protect her?

They walked across the lawn together silently, their footsteps silenced by the grass. And even after they entered the dark forest, he didn't release her. She should not be going with him. She should make an excuse. She wouldn't even require an excuse. This was most unacceptable.

"I want to show you something." He seemed to have a specific destination in mind as he weaved her along a haphazard path. "This way." He held a finger up to his lips and then ducked in-between some thick brush. Not knowing where he was leading them, or what she would find there, she tiptoed quietly behind.

Moonlight slanted in between the branches above, shining on the trunk of a tree about eight feet away from her. Chiseled into the trunk, someone had created a large cavity. She peered closer and smiled. Nestled there was a cluster of leaves and twigs that cradled three tiny birds and two shiny eggs. One of the eggs was cracked, with obvious activity occurring inside. A larger bird—she must be the mother—stood guard, perched on the very edge of the nest.

Eliza glanced over at Henry and lifted her brows. "Shouldn't they have hatched by now?" Already it was late summer. Eggs hatched in the early spring.

Henry merely shrugged but then lifted a finger to his lips. "Mama sees you," he whispered, drawing her backward.

"Can we watch? I don't want to scare her."

His hand squeezed hers reassuringly. "We won't if we keep our distance. Its why I brought you here."

After a quick glance around them, Henry surprised her by

dropping to one knee. "Your chair, my lady." He indicated the bench of his leg. "This might take a while." When she hesitated, he added, "It's just that I know you've spent all day on your feet. Would you rather return to the inn?"

She did not want to return to the inn. Eliza shook her head and then putting one hand on his shoulder, dropped onto his leg.

His scent, his warmth, washed over her. She'd not been this close to him before and her thoughts seemed to tumble and swirl. Eliza turned her gaze to where she could just see the egg that was breaking apart, but it was hard to focus on anything but the man beside her—beneath her—all around her.

"I came across it while I was out earlier this evening. I'm glad they haven't all hatched yet." Eliza felt the whisper of his breath along her cheek sending a tremble through her.

"Are you cold?"

She was not. It was late summer.

"Yes," she answered, suddenly feeling vulnerable. How did a person's skin ache to be touched? How had she lost control of the butterflies jumping in her belly?

His response was to pull her closer to his chest, which did nothing to reestablish her equilibrium.

"They are woodpeckers," he whispered again.

Eliza nodded as she watched a tiny beak push away another small piece of shell. It had been sweet of Henry to think of her —to bring her to witness something so special.

He'd been nothing but kind since arriving in Misty Brooke. As she stared at the nest, she suddenly felt like crying. When had Matthew stopped treating her with kindness? Why did she no longer ache to be held by him?

"Eliza?" Henry dipped his head so that he could look at her. "Are you all right? You are crying?" The concern on his face was nearly her undoing.

She closed her eyes and the tear she'd been holding back

slid down her cheek. "I am scared," she whispered. She hadn't even realized the truth until she spoke the words aloud.

"What are you afraid of?" Tenderness had crept into his voice.

She shook her head. "It's nothing. I shouldn't say anything. I'm simply being weepy."

Henry sat silent for a moment. And then. "We are friends. Are we not? You can talk to me. Perhaps if you speak your fears aloud, you'll understand them better."

And somehow, she found her face buried in his chest. "I know it's probably nothing but I—I have cold feet. I think. I'm beginning to wonder if I'm doing the right thing. But it is too late. My parents would be devastated, and my brother would be humiliated. I'm likely just being silly."

Henry's hand was on her hair. His throat moved when he swallowed hard. "Eliza," he spoke her name. "You are not being silly. If I was that fiancé of yours, I'd not allow you to sit outside with another man. I'd not spend my evenings playing cards in the tap room if you were nearby. Good God, I'd never leave you alone on a warm summer night."

"What *would* you do?" She should not have asked such a question. And yet, she lifted her head so that she could see his eyes when he answered it.

"Every moment is a gift. Do you know that? Everything can be taken away in the blink of an eye." He stared back at her. "If I were your fiancé…," his voice broke.

Eliza parted her lips, her entire body on the verge of trembling. She reached a hand up to his jaw and settled it there. The moonlight softened his hawk-like features so that she nearly lost herself in his eyes. She barely knew this man. Why had he come into her life? For what purpose? She slid her hand up and back and threaded his silky black hair through her fingers.

"If I was your fiancé, I would do this." Henry leaned forward and placed his mouth upon hers. So softly at first, and then more demanding. When his tongue slid past her lips, something ignited inside of her. It was as though she'd been asleep for a very long time and was finally being awoken. Both of her hands clutched at his hair now, delighting in the springy thickness.

A low groan emerged from him and thrummed into her mouth, down to her chest.

Who was Henry Fairchild? Eliza felt as though she'd been waiting for him her entire life. His tongue swept around the crevasses of her mouth, causing her to squeeze her thighs together.

She wanted him.

She wanted Henry Fairchild.

When he ended the kiss, the trembling she'd been holding back took hold of her. His breathing labored the same as hers.

He tucked her head beneath his chin. "Eliza." His voice sounded pained.

The fear she'd experienced a moment before had grown and exploded into a thousand little pieces. She wasn't quite sure what had replaced it. And she wasn't quite sure if she ought to be more afraid now than ever before.

CHAPTER ONE

TWELVE YEARS LATER

"Now remember, Thomas, Mrs. Pope will be coming by to cook your dinner each night. She said she'd bake bread when you run out and I've made it quite clear to her that you prefer stews over soups. And if you've need of anything before church services, Beatrice Long promised she would make herself available." Eliza stifled the urge to bite her nails as she contemplated anything that she might have forgotten. "Are you certain you can wash your own shirts? Perhaps I oughtn't go after—"

"I'm a grown man, not a child, Eliza. I can take care of myself." Thomas, her dear brother, shook his head as he assisted her into the coach that waited to drive her to the Christmas House Party to which she'd been invited. It was a long day's drive away and she wouldn't be returning to the vicarage for nearly a fortnight.

His words were meant to reassure her. No, he was not a child, nor was she. But as an aging spinster, she had no business attending parties and dances. She'd changed her mind a dozen times before responding to the letter that had come along with Olivia's invitation, and then she'd changed it a dozen more after she'd responded with her acceptance.

"I shouldn't go. Perhaps I will stay—"

"You are going, Eliza. You've done nothing but take care of me, the vicarage and this parish for too long. You deserve some time to yourself. Besides, John here has driven all the way from Sky Manor to collect you. It would be inconsiderate of you to change your mind now."

"You're right. Of course, you are right." She turned and embraced her brother one last time before climbing into the private carriage sent by the Earl and Countess of Kingsley. Her brother was dearer to her than she could ever say. When even her own parents had shunned her, he'd taken her in. "I will miss you though." She leaned out the door. "Happy Christmas Thomas!"

"You'll be home soon enough, and you will tell me all about this grand house party. We will laugh that you ever thought to remain at home."

He closed the door firmly behind her, waving as she blew him a kiss. He did not seem overly sad at her departure. Perhaps he looked forward to having the vicarage to himself. No one to interrupt his reading, no one to remind him to wear his scarf when he walked to the church in the cold.

Eliza sat back and closed her eyes. She had not traveled more than ten miles from the vicarage in over a decade. And she was to be gone for nearly a fortnight! Over the holidays no less!

She bit her lip and watched outside the window as they left the familiar village of Misty Brooke behind. This wasn't really all that great of an adventure. It wasn't as though she was boarding a ship to the America's for heaven's sake. By the time the driver stopped to change out the horses, she was berating herself for being such a ninny. Seeing new faces for the first time in ages made her think that perhaps she'd waited too long to spread her wings. She was almost thirty. Yes, she was firmly on the shelf but that didn't mean she must stop seeking out new experiences.

Visiting Olivia Fellowes was the perfect opportunity to remind herself that a world existed outside of Misty Brooke. She could have friends outside of the vicarage—people to whom she could write letters, people who traveled and did not think of her only as the vicar's sister. The thought ought to have cheered her, but pessimism set in quickly. If anyone learned of her past… She shuddered.

The other guests at the party would be people of quality and Eliza just barely laid claim to gentility. Her father was the son of a vicar and her mother had boasted of having a second cousin who was a baronet.

Snowflakes began drifting from the sky and in no time the flurries were rushing all around them. A strong gust of wind pushed against the carriage and Eliza grasped the strap hanging from the ceiling. Just as she thought to pound on the wall and suggest they turn around, Coachman John slid open the window that opened to the driver's box. Flakes of snow whipped their way inside through the small opening causing Eliza to huddle deeper in her coat.

"We shouldn't travel in this, but not to worry, Miss Cline. There's an inn right ahead. Best to stop and wait out the storm rather than risk sliding off the road."

"Yes." She shouted back in agreement, picturing them careening down a hill, or into a ravine. "I think that would be best."

She should have remained at the vicarage. Eliza clutched the strap hanging from the ceiling and braced herself for certain death.

. . .

The Hen and Hog Inn had but a few rooms left. After paying the inn keeper and carrying her small valise up the narrow stairs, she found herself pleasantly surprised when she unlocked the door and pushed it open. The space was rather large, as was the bed. She washed her hands and face and then drifted around, examining the small desk, the wardrobe, and she even discovered a trundle stored beneath the tall bed. This required all of seventeen minutes.

She stared at the clock on the mantle and frowned. It was barely past noon. She had a long day ahead of her and she had not thought to bring along a book to read.

Foolish.

She could not sit inside doing nothing for the remainder of the day, she would drive herself mad. Gathering her shawl and her reticule, she stopped to check herself in the mirror. Her tight chignon remained intact, just a few brownish wisps of hairs had escaped, and her dress, although slightly wrinkled, still appeared somewhat fresh. And then she grimaced at herself. Her appearance did not really matter so long as she was clean and proper.

The tap room was not crowded so she easily located a table and chair by the window. At least she could watch the storm from here, or any new guests who checked in. She slowly slid her gaze around the room until it landed on some men sitting at a long table. The oldest of the group looked as though he'd had a hard life, his skin ruddy and thick. The three younger men with him might be related. They conversed quietly as they drank their ale.

A family occupied the other long table farther away. The children seemed to be well behaved as they tore off pieces of bread and sipped what looked to be cups of chocolate. They did not appear to be poor but neither did they seem to be well off.

They laughed and smiled with one another. The husband

occasionally placed a hand around his wife's not-so-slim waist.

They looked happy.

Eliza had once thought she'd have a family.

A maid appeared and Eliza waved to get her attention in order to ask for some hot tea. As the woman approached, Eliza wondered if the maid was also required to clean the rooms.

She shuddered.

She hadn't set foot inside of an inn since that last horrid, horrid day at the Dog and Pudding Pot. "Does the inn fill up often?" Eliza asked the maid, feeling an odd connection with her.

"Almost every night in the warmer months, and in springtime. But the winters are normally slow." And then she winked. "A good storm like this one helps though. Are you sure you don't want something to eat with your tea?"

Eliza shook her head.

Sitting in such surroundings unearthed a flood of unwanted memories. Had Eliza made different choices; her life would be so very different. As it was, another woman toiled at the Dog and Pudding alongside Matthew's mother. Mr. Wilson had passed a few years back.

Last she heard the couple had been blessed with six healthy children. It wasn't as though Eliza could avoid them. They attended church regularly but on the few occasions Eliza had caught the young Mrs. Wilson staring at her, the woman had quickly averted her gaze. Matthew, nor his wife, nor his mother ever acknowledged her. They never spoke to her. They were, however, cordial to Thomas. After all, he was the vicar. They hardly had a choice. It had taken a few years before anyone in the parish had warmed to Eliza.

Her shame had been a very public matter.

After consuming two cups of the strong hot brew, Eliza sighed and slumped so that her forehead rested against the cold glass. Time was sure to pass slowly. A woman traveling alone could not simply start up a conversation with a stranger and so she had only herself for company.

She ought to be excited to attend Olivia's party but for all the upheaval, she simply felt deflated, tired.

Old.

A fire burned in the corner of the taproom, and tonight she would sleep in a warm and clean bed.

She ought to be content. She ought to be grateful for all that she had.

Living and working with her brother Thomas at the vicarage provided her with all the fulfillment she ought to have ever sought. She helped feed the poor and care for the sick. She heard all the latest gossip...

But something was missing. At the age of nine and twenty, Eliza admitted to herself that she wanted...

More.

And sitting here with nothing to do but worry, she had nothing else to do but examine this discontent. She'd had her chance long ago. She'd risked everything thinking she'd found that 'more' she now dreamed of and look how that turned out.

She'd not risk her good standing again.

But there were moments--she touched her fingers to her lips.

Moments when she'd awaken from a dream and find herself aching. Moments she simply wished...

Her conscience chastised her for such an ungrateful thought.

Sitting here, in a room full of strangers, a heated blush worked its way up her neck and into her cheeks at the thought that anyone could read her thoughts or know the contents of those scandalous dreams.

One glance around emphasized all too well how ridiculous it was for her to blush.

No one ever even looked at her. They looked past her.

But they did not see Eliza Cline, the person.

Looking as she did, wearing her drab gown and a pair of spectacles perched atop her nose, she might as well have been invisible. And that was fine. It was just fine.

People saw her, of course they saw her. They saw her for what she could do for others, for her good deeds and the baskets of rations she delivered to those in need.

She removed her spectacles and wiped at the corner of one of her eyes.

The holidays loomed a week away and instead of feeling excitement for all of her blessings, she had fallen into a melancholy. Another year gone by.

Eliza stared down at her hands. She would never have a family. A husband. Someone who would hold her at night, who would be there when she awoke. Someone who would…

One of her eyelashes lay on the back of her hand. Feeling silly, she closed her eyes, made an impossible wish and then blew it off.

And then ruefully smiled at herself.

Interrupting her indulgent musings, an elegant coach pulled by four beautiful horses came to a stop just outside her window. The uniformed driver and outriders jumped down and hastily brushed snow off of their hats and coats before disappearing from her sight, presumably to assist the travelers out of the carriage. Eliza leaned forward but only got a glimpse of the passengers before the door to the inn burst open and a well-dressed young man entered along with a burst of flurries and cold air. Behind him scurried a dark-haired girl of perhaps five and ten and another mob-capped lady, presumably her companion or maid. Eliza donned her spectacles quickly, feeling self-conscious but also wanting to see who the newcomers might be.

The innkeeper scowled at first but upon seeing another

older gentleman wearing a greatcoat with many layers follow the young people inside, he became all that was welcoming. The new arrivals were obviously quality.

The other patrons, who had been openly inspecting them, quickly lost interest and turned their attention back to one another and their pints without comment.

Nobody noticed Eliza, she remained invisible to those surrounding her. She'd been invisible for a very long time...

Since the newcomers all had their backs turned to her, she had no reason to feign disinterest. The two men were of similar height, but the taller man's shoulders stretched slightly wider and he held himself with more...

She couldn't decide. Arrogance? Confidence? No, something else—maturity, wisdom. He must be the elder of the two.

The younger removed his hat and, without thought to anyone around him, shook it so that the snow scattered. He then brushed at his shoulders with the same casual aplomb.

"Have a care, Bartholomew." The younger girl stepped away from the brash young man. "My coat's already wet enough."

"Then a few more snowflakes shouldn't bother you." He must be her brother. Only siblings spoke so frankly to one another.

The well-dressed young woman scowled and lifted her chin. She glanced around and what she saw only deepened her frown. She was obviously of the opinion that she was far too good for her present surroundings.

It was easy to dismiss particular blessings at such a young age.

"You're in luck, My Lord," the innkeeper addressed the taller man, who'd also removed his hat. He ran a hand through his hair in an attempt to bring it under control. It was thick and black, sprinkled with just enough silver to be interesting. Eliza tugged her shawl more tightly around her shoulders as a sense of unease ran through her.

His air of authority lent himself to be either father or uncle to the other two... perhaps a much older brother. "We have one available room left to let. Filling up quick-like with the storm."

"But we need two rooms, Papa!" The girl stepped up to the desk. Eliza studied her profile. Even from the distant vantage point, some ten feet away, she could make out the girl's pouting lips.

Eliza glanced back out the window, ignoring the sensation that the hair on the back of her neck was standing on end. She was in a strange place, amongst strangers, of course she would feel a bit out of sorts—in foul weather, no less.

The yard was hardly visible now, the innocent-looking flakes having turned to a scurrying whirlwind of white. No one would last long outside in what was quickly transforming into a blizzard.

And just before Christmas. How appropriate, she thought cynically. The one and only time she'd ever been invited to a holiday celebration, snow had made such an inconvenient appearance.

Eliza ought to be cheered by it.

Olivia would likely have all of them building snowmen and having snow wars. Her dear friend had married well and was graciously hosting the Christmas party at her husband's grand country estate.

At least, Eliza assumed it would be grand, as her newlywed friend's husband was an earl.

"If you could be so kind as to check again, good sir. My daughter and her maid require private quarters."

Eliza turned back to watch the scenario at the counter, a prickle of awareness spreading up her spine. There was something familiar about the man's voice, but she could not put her finger on it.

The flustered innkeeper shuffled through some papers but continued to shake his head in a discouraging manner. "I'm quite certain… unless I were to put out one of the guests who's already arrived..."

The girl nodded, but her father shook his head. "That will not be necessary. If there are some cots lying about somewhere…"

That prickle turned to a most unusual combination of excitement and mortification.

Add to that regret and terror. In fact, more terror than anything else.

It could not be.

Ah, yes, she had known the possibility existed that she'd see him again, although she'd considered the event highly unlikely. Part of her wanted to hide, and yet, she twisted her mouth into a grimace. He would not look at her.

Would he even remember?

"I've a small mudroom in back where we can set up two cots." The innkeeper would not wish to lose these paying guests.

"Father!" The younger man was not at all agreeable with such a plan. "I'm not sleeping on a cot as though we're common vagrants."

"You'll do as I say." The older man's voice cut him off in a cold manner she'd not heard from him before.

It was him. She was certain of it. These young people were his *children*.

"Charlotte and Mrs. Blake will take the available chamber, and you can either sleep on the cot or in the stables. It is up to you."

Eliza wondered that the boy thought it fair to turn out another guest, one who'd arrived before himself, of the room they'd already let. She pinched her lips together.

They were a wealthy family, nobility even. He'd told her he was the second son of a baron. A long time ago.

All was not amiable amongst them, however: father, son,

and daughter. A strained discontent was quite apparent to her in just the few minutes she'd observed.

"We'll take the room. You do have private dining quarters, I assume?" he addressed the innkeeper once again.

"Of course, My Lord. Of course." Ah, so he was no longer a mere second son but a lord himself.

And just then, the gentleman glanced over his shoulder. Eliza inhaled sharply.

The same ebony hair, but now with a hint of gray, hawkish features, emerald eyes, a firm chin slightly shadowed by a day's growth of beard.

He was older but no less handsome than he'd been twelve years ago. His eyes no longer twinkled with laughter, though, and his mouth was set in a tight line.

But even if his appearance had changed drastically, she would know him.

Henry Fairchild.

CHAPTER TWO

THE FAIRCHILDS

Keeping her dignity, but also experiencing outrage and a desire to make herself known, she pushed back her chair and crossed the room.

"Excuse me." She cleared her throat when her voice came out sounding hoarse and dry.

When no one acknowledged her, some of her confidence fled, but she cleared her throat again. "I'd be more than happy to share my chamber with your daughter and her maid," she volunteered. "So that you and your son may have a bed." Her room was large, and it was the Christian thing to do. In addition to that, it was almost Christmas.

What was she doing?

She did not wish to remain invisible today.

The younger man turned with a smile. For a moment a single butterfly fluttered in her chest. He looked so very much like his father.

Perhaps she was a fool for drawing attention to herself. Even more so for giving up her privacy. She had no idea how long they would all be stuck here. For all she knew, the storm could go on for days, making travel impossible.

"Look here, Father." The young man found her suggestion most convenient.

And at last, he turned to acknowledge Eliza. Her blood ran cold and hot at the same time beneath his gaze.

"Do I know you, Miss...?" He was scowling as he raised a monocle to one eye. The creases around his mouth showed the twelve years that had passed. He seemed the same but... different.

"Miss Cline. Miss Eliza Cline," she prompted. "From Misty Brooke, the Dog and Pudding Pot." She could tell he was searching his memory, and then... there it was.

The dawn of recollection.

She curtsied in her plain dress with her ugly brown shawl wrapped around her shoulders. As she lifted her head, she was forced to push the spectacles higher upon her nose. She hadn't needed them until a few years ago. If she thought he looked older, what on earth must he think when he looked at her?

And then she'd gone and reminded him that she'd once been in service. She was not ashamed of it. She might be in an even worse position if not for her brother.

He made a quick bow but then glanced at his daughter when she tugged at his sleeve.

"I don't want to share a room with a stranger, Papa." Her eyes slid toward Eliza. "My gratitude, all the same."

"You are Mr. Fairchild, are you not?" Eliza demanded his attention once again. But of course, he was no longer a mere mister. "We were acquainted some time ago—"

"I am aware." He cut her off, staring at her with something of a pained expression.

For years, Eliza had wished for the opportunity to rail at him. She'd wanted to demand answers—demand an explanation that could somehow allow her to make sense of it all. With him standing before her now, though, she merely wished to be acknowledged.

"He is not Mr. Fairchild, madam. He is Lord Crestwood." The young girl informed her as though offended.

"But we are the Fairchilds." The young man scowled in his sister's direction. "Father, Miss Cline's offer provides the best solution," he added cajolingly.

"Miss Cline." *Lord Crestwood* cocked one eyebrow and then the left side of his mouth lifted as though he'd forgotten how to smile. "You may withdraw your kind offer, if you'd like. If you do not, I'm afraid I'm going to take you up on it, on behalf of my most ill-mannered offspring."

Eliza swallowed hard. He'd smiled at her before, with both corners of his mouth. Oh, what that smile had done to her twelve years ago.

She ought to withdraw the offer. Have as little as possible to do with this man. But she shook her head. The large chamber she'd been given boasted a bed, easily large enough for two, and also a trundle for the maid. Sharing her room, she reminded herself again, was the *Christian* thing to do.

And Eliza always did the Christian thing, what with being a vicar's sister, and all...

"I will not withdraw it." She tightened her lips so as not to respond to his good looks and charm. Lord Crestwood was obviously married—with children—and then a horrific understanding slowly crept into her conscience—much as a snake might slither out from under a rock.

These two young people were *his children* and were far older than the age of two and ten.

Unease swirled around her brain as the magnitude of these circumstances hit her with more force than the wind and snow would have had she gone dashing outside.

His children who were almost grown, around the age of fifteen and older, she'd guess. Which meant he was married.

Which meant he had been married twelve years ago.

And that meant that not only had she fornicated outside the bonds of matrimony, but she had committed adultery.

She'd lain with a married man!

* * *

HENRY FAIRCHILD, Baron Crestwood, remembered her the moment she'd spoken her name. He'd truly looked at her then, and her eyes had jolted him into the past.

A past that tainted his honor. A bittersweet time that he'd both dreamt about but also suffered nightmares over. She'd been so young, and he'd been... He swallowed hard.

The self-loathing he felt was an old friend. He'd embraced it for so long it was now a part of him.

She'd barely been ten and eight and he'd easily charmed her. When he'd complimented her eyes, she'd insisted they were plain, as brown could often be. He'd found them sultry and inviting, like chocolate or coffee. They stood out to him even from behind the metal-rimmed spectacles she now wore. Thick lashes framed her eyes, contrasting starkly with her alabaster skin.

To the undiscerning observer, she was quite forgettable.

Years ago, he'd found Eliza Cline to be a beauty in hiding. Dragging his eyes up and down her drab clothing and unimaginative hairstyle, he suspected this was still the case.

"Papa," Charlotte, his daughter of ten and six, wailed softly. "I don't—"

"Charlotte, this is Miss Eliza Cline. Miss Cline, my daughter, Miss Charlotte Fairchild. Bartholomew, Miss Cline. Miss Cline, my son, Bartholomew Fairchild."

The woman he'd never expected to see again, let alone introduce to his children, blinked a few times and then greeted his less than mannerly offspring. She then turned to acknowledge Charlotte's maid, Mrs. Blake, with some reserve.

The woman who was his greatest regret, turned toward his daughter. "If you are ready now, I'll show you to my chamber."

Charlotte gave him one last pleading look but then dropped her lashes at his unrelenting stare.

Her surname had not changed. When he'd seen her last, she had been engaged to be married.

Henry clenched his jaw. The fiancé had broken it off then.

He'd wondered.

Miss Cline turned to lead his daughter and her maid upstairs, and he stopped her with his question. "You will join us for dinner? Of course?" It was the least he could do as she was giving up her privacy.

She glanced over her shoulder with narrowed eyes. If she harbored ill will, why had she offered to share her chamber?

But then her chin dipped in acquiescence.

Henry pinched his jaw. He'd bedded her twelve years ago and when she'd expected his protection, he'd had nothing to offer her. Less than nothing. A burning sensation had him rubbing his clenched fist over his chest.

They'd been caught in a most inappropriate situation, by her fiancé, and Henry had had the gall to become annoyed.

His actions had been appalling, unforgivable.

What a villain he'd been. A selfish, deplorable villain.

And yet, he'd not been himself. Even now, he remembered feeling as though he'd been watching somebody else in his place... Which was no excuse...

"The key, My Lord." The innkeeper's voice jolted him from such unsettling memories.

Henry turned, signed the register, and indicated for Bartholomew to follow him up the narrow staircase. He'd share a room with his son this night. Hopefully, the weather would clear, and they could make the remainder of their journey tomorrow morning.

He wasn't sure quite what he would say to Miss Cline if he

found himself alone with her. Likely, she'd have some angry words to hurl at his deserving head.

He'd ruined her.

CHAPTER THREE

REMORSE

Miss Charlotte Fairchild had yet to acknowledge or thank Eliza in any way. Shortly after they arrived at Eliza's room, manservants appeared with the young woman's trunk and smaller valise. The girl threw herself across the bed, facedown, while Mrs. Blake went to work unpacking a few lovely gowns and draping them over the only chair in the room.

This had been a mistake. Eliza berated herself for allowing her charitable inclinations to put her in this situation.

And yet, she could not any ill will toward his children. The thought shook her.

She didn't know what to feel. How could any of this be real? Her emotions were so confused as to be almost numb. It was as though she'd stepped into a different world as the reality of her past shifted into something so… unthinkable.

Edging to the bed, Eliza lowered herself onto the corner of the mattress. "If it hadn't made travel impossible, I'd be more than happy with snow over the holidays. Are you on your way to celebrate Christmas with family?" Eliza spoke to the back of the girl's head.

"Arousrarty," Miss Fairchild mumbled into the pillow.

"A house party?" Eliza hated sullenness, and yet she remembered the angst one experienced at such an age. "That sounds quite festive." But she could not contain herself from asking, "Are you meeting your mother there?"

The girl rolled over and stared at her blankly, escaped strands of dark hair covering parts of her face. "My mother is dead."

Oh, dear! Why hadn't she thought of this? One ought never to make such assumptions. "I'm sorry." Eliza's own parents were still alive. As far as she knew. Presumably, she and Thomas would have been notified had one of them passed.

"Don't be. It's not as though she made a big difference in my life—"

Mrs. Blake made a few disapproving sounds.

"Well, it's true." Miss Fairchild's gaze flicked toward the maid.

"I would imagine one would miss what a mother provides, even if one doesn't recognize it." Eliza reached over to the small table by the bed to absentmindedly examine the contents of her reticule.

Had Lord Crestwood's wife had been alive at the time she'd known him? For a moment, she hoped the woman had died in childbirth—not that she wished any woman such a horrible and tragic death, nor that she'd wished his children never to have known their mother, but that she'd wished she'd not committed adultery twelve years ago.

Was it possible?

Following his abrupt departure, she'd regarded him as a bounder and a rake, but this! She never would have imagined. Not once had he given her any indication…

How could this be happening? Her stomach lurched. She had to be certain.

"You must be coming out soon, Miss Fairchild. Are you yet

six and ten?" The girl was older than twelve, but Eliza must be certain.

"Nearly. I will be in a few weeks, but my father is making me wait two years before taking me to London. He treats me like a child!"

Oh, and, of course, the son was even older. That meant the woman had been quite alive when Eliza had known him.

It was worse than she ever could have imagined. She would have liked to bury her own face upon that pillow alongside Miss Fairchild.

His grown daughter.

Not only had he had a wife, but he'd also had a family!

Eliza blinked away tears of anger, raging inside all the while she sat placidly upon the bed with her back straight and her lips pinched together tightly.

Suddenly, the room seemed to be closing in from all sides. She could not sit here a second longer.

She burst from the bed and, without further comment, located her coat and gloves.

"Surely, you aren't going outside, miss?" Mrs. Blake looked at her in astonishment.

"I... I..." How could she explain herself? "I have need of some air."

"But you'll catch your death!" The maid glanced out the window. If anything, the storm had strengthened. She could barely make out the brown of the stable across the yard.

Eliza half stumbled toward the door. "I'll only be a moment."

And then she was rushing through the tight corridor outside the various chambers. Head down, she descended the stairs, crossed through the taproom, and slipped outside, grateful for once for her invisibility.

The wind bit into her cheeks and tugged at her coat and

hair the instant she stepped away from the building. But she didn't care. She deserved it.

She'd held onto those passion filled memories. She'd dreamt of him, longed for him. She'd made excuses for him despite his abandonment. For a time, she'd mourned him, assuming that he must have died.

If he'd yet lived, surely, he would have come back to her.

Because the man she'd thought she'd known would not have hurt her the way he had. In the wake of his departure, her life had turned upside down.

Such memories could only curse her now.

He'd been married! She'd allowed him to make love to her and all along, he'd had a wife!

A copse of trees beckoned from behind the Inn. Her feet, somewhat protected by well-worn but practical half-boots, did not feel the cold. Only a few inches of snow had as of yet accumulated.

With her eyes focused on a perfectly shaped evergreen, she tripped her way forward to escape any eyes that might have seen her flight. If only she could flee this day as well. Or skip over it, pretend it never happened.

If only she could flee from herself!

She increased her pace, practically running until she was safely out of sight of the windows overlooking the yard. She picked her way through the trees until she found a thick, solid trunk with little brush at its base that would support her.

Where she proceeded to bend over and lose what was surely the entire contents of her stomach. The retching sounds roared in her ears. Eyes closed, she half-sobbed with each convulsion.

She hated him. Oh, how she hated him. He was evil.

I am evil!

She choked on another sob.

Clutching her abdomen with one hand, supporting herself

against the tree with her other, she spit onto the ground in an attempt to remove the taste of bile from her mouth.

She'd had relations with a married man outside of wedlock.

Twelve years ago!

She'd known her behavior had been bad enough but to learn he'd been married…

Her stomach convulsed again but nothing remained to expel. Tears streamed down her face now. Tears she'd not even realized she'd shed.

Leaning forward, she allowed the sharp edges of the bark to press into the top of her head. Cold seeped through her shoes and a gust of wind blew right through her wool coat, shawl, dress, and underclothes.

He'd asked… no, he'd essentially *demanded* she join him and his children for the evening meal. And she'd not refused.

Oh, how she hated that she'd grown so utterly accustomed to putting the wishes of others before her own.

"Miss Cline?"

Eliza drew in a deep breath. Of course, now, he would come upon her in such humiliating circumstances.

"Leave me, please." Her voice sounded hoarse, practically a whisper.

A crisp white linen handkerchief appeared before her, clasped in those long, elegant fingers of his.

"I cannot allow you to remain outside." He opened his hand, encouraging her to take the slip of material. On a sigh, she reluctantly accepted it and dabbed the linen against her lips, still bending over and quite unwilling to look him in the face.

"I imagine you hate me about now." That same languid voice she remembered from so long ago dripped from his mouth. "With good reason."

"You had a wife." The words burned her throat, and she forced herself to stifle another sob that threatened to escape. "A wife!" At last, she turned her head and met his gaze.

She hadn't realized he was crouching beside her, nor that his face would be so close to hers. Those hawkish features of his, not to mention his stunning green eyes, were mere inches from her own.

He held her stare steadily and nodded.

"I hate you. I will hate you forever." She'd never said those words to another living person. And yet they were also directed inward. She hated everything about herself at that moment. Why did he have to show up here, of all places, with his beautiful but spoiled children?

She noticed a movement in his throat, as though he were swallowing her hatred.

His hand touched her back, and she flinched out of his reach.

But then it settled there again, and she had nowhere to go.

She moaned, and he pulled his hand away.

"Please come back inside," he begged, sounding resigned. "I cannot leave you out here in the cold like this."

She'd given him her body. Although she'd been working at the inn, she had been a gently bred young lady. "You had no difficulty leaving me before. Now, I understand why. You had a wife to return to. *A wife and two children!* I'm no responsibility of yours."

If only she could remain outside forever. Allow the cold to penetrate her body as much as her guilt had taken over her soul. Disappear completely.

But such thoughts were evil.

She couldn't wallow in self-pity forever. Others depended upon her. Or did they?

"I cannot walk through a room full of strangers looking like this," she said when he did not respond to her accusation. She must look a fright, with tree bark in her hair and splotches of red streaking her face.

A heavy coat dropped onto her shoulders.

Ah, the irony. He would protect her from a blizzard now, when he'd…

But the worst of it all was that she'd been equally to blame. She had known it was wrong. She'd been *engaged!* Everything she'd ever learned in life had promised her she'd suffer for such poor judgment.

Earlier today, she'd wished for something more in her life. She had to learn to be careful of what she wished for.

She inhaled and the scent of man, the scent of such an *elegant masculine gentleman,* engulfed her senses, reminding her partly of why she'd given herself to him in the first place. What kind of woman was she?

She shivered in the warmth left over from his body.

Eliza could not change the past any more than she could change her current circumstances.

She wiped her mouth again with his handkerchief. "I do not require your coat." She rose to her full height. He pushed himself from his haunches and managed to somehow appear as equally formal and handsome as before he'd come out into the storm.

Except for the lock of hair that now swept along his cheek and jaw, seeming to emphasize his austere features all the more.

A blast of wind ripped between the trees, and she swayed, her knees nearly buckling.

"Steady there." This time, when he took hold of her arm, she hadn't the strength to push him away. Her moment of revulsion having left her weakened.

She hated feeling weak. She was Miss Eliza Cline—dependable, strong, able to step in whenever parishioners were in need.

Eliza Cline was not this pathetic, scandalous woman who'd run recklessly into a blizzard.

"I am fine." She forced her shoulders back.

It wasn't that anyone else would know or suspect what she'd done. But... knowing herself was bad enough.

And God knew.

She shuddered but made herself take one step, and then another.

"Eliza! Miss Cline!" His voice halted her. If he deigned to apologize or make some excuse or reason for omitting such pertinent information when they'd been acquainted before, she was going to scream.

This was not something she could forgive.

"What?" she answered impatiently, freezing in place.

"The inn is this way."

She lifted her chin and made an attempt to find her bearings. The snow was falling so thick now that she could barely make out the shadow of the building she'd fled from. If he hadn't followed her, she might have simply wandered off to nowhere, never to be heard from again.

And no one would have been the wiser.

She blinked at her maudlin thoughts but turned and walked in the direction he indicated. Her feet were freezing but other than that, she only felt emptiness.

He did not attempt to touch her as they trekked through accumulating snow. Upon reaching the covered porch at the entrance, Eliza shrugged out of his coat and numbly handed it over. White flakes covered his hair and shoulders. His face was grim.

Apparently, he, too, realized that any sort of apology could never be accepted. What he'd done was unforgivable. She was relieved he realized this.

She would not thank him for coming after her, nor for the use of his coat. Looking at him only managed to rebuke her for what she'd done.

"I'll see you at supper," he reminded her.

She nodded. And sometime in the future, she'd meet him in hell.

* * *

HENRY WAITED OUTSIDE LONG after Miss Cline left him standing there. He'd been the one to walk away twelve years ago.

He'd been traveling through Misty Brookes and stopped at… what had she called it, oh, yes—The Dog and Pudding Pot—when he'd first met her. She'd been open and friendly when he'd wanted conversation. She'd surprised him with her intelligence and profound opinions. She'd also been engaged to marry the innkeeper's son. Henry could not remember the man's name; he barely remembered how he'd even arrived in that fateful village; he'd been so mired in despair from what he'd learned of his wife's condition.

That the young girl who made him laugh had belonged to another man and to Henry, that had been of no consequence. Neither had he considered that he had nothing to offer her. He'd pretended to be a bachelor, a younger brother to himself. He'd pretended his troubles never existed and that he was merely a young man returning from a leisurely trip to London.

He'd filled her head with lies.

He'd flirted with her, dazzled her with his fine speech and aristocratic airs. Ah, yes, what an ass he'd been. And when he'd sensed that she was falling in love with him, he'd done nothing to dissuade her. In fact, he'd encouraged her.

And then he'd seduced her.

Henry would shoot any man who dared a sideways glance at his own daughter, let alone acted in the manner that he had.

It wasn't that he hadn't cared for Eliza… Miss Cline… in his own selfish way. She'd been like a balm to his soul at the time. He'd imagined he could love her while it suited him. Since God had cast him into a living hell with Francine's injury, he'd believed he could strike back at life however he'd liked.

Remorse had come later, when he'd gone home and sat with Francine that first night.

A combination of self-disgust and bitter regret had moved into his soul.

It had yet to depart.

He'd hurt Miss Cline in the worst way and betrayed his wife at the same time. Francine had been lost within herself, lost to reality, and even though he'd confessed, she'd only nodded with that empty look in her eyes.

But he'd abandoned Miss Cline to suffer the consequences.

Henry had been the cause of her broken engagement, and in turn, she had never married. If her fiancé had jilted her it was possible their affair had been exposed. What other penalties had she endured?

No wonder she'd had to run into the forest to vomit. He deserved her hatred. He deserved far worse than that.

A whipping gust of wind reminded him he was standing outside in freezing weather. He brushed the snow off his head. Nothing he could do about it now. It was obvious she had no desire for him to make an apology. No apology could suffice.

She'd recoiled from his touch.

Stepping inside, he determined he would make certain she had all that was needed for her stay at this infernal inn. And then they'd go their separate ways.

He could not change the past. But she could rely on him to be the utmost gentleman in the present.

CHAPTER FOUR

DINNER CONVERSATION

Eliza should have chosen to dine in the taproom amongst the other guests; she would have been a thousand times more comfortable. She'd have been ignored, as usual, and not been concerned about her appearance or making conversation.

Instead, she sat in Lord Crestwood's private dining quarters, a warm fire burning in the corner and several candles flickering in the center of the table, feeling most out of place.

Miss Charlotte Fairchild sat morosely playing with her soup. A nervous energy emanated from Lord Crestwood's son, who sat bouncing one knee unpleasantly after consuming his own soup in less than two minutes.

Lord Crestwood seemed to be doing his best to ignore them all.

The soup had been watered down. Eliza speculated that the innkeepers hadn't been prepared for such a full establishment and needed to stretch supplies somewhat. It was only right, however, to appreciate what was set before her.

When one of the maids entered to serve a few loaves of bread, Eliza didn't miss the furtive glances exchanged between the very young woman and young Mr. Fairchild. Lord Crestwood's son had obviously already charmed the woman, if her fluttering lashes and smile were anything to go by.

Eliza pinched her lips together.

Like father, like son.

This was too hard. How could she not remember the past with him sitting just a few feet across from her?

Just as his son was now, Henry had been incredibly handsome. She'd known he had been older than her. She hadn't stood a chance against such charm, not to mention that he'd been born into the aristocracy! He'd been attractive in every way imaginable. He'd asked her opinion on matters that meant something to her. It had been refreshing to discuss philosophy, history and literature instead of chamber pots and laundry. And he'd listened to her. And she had listened to him.

He'd told her she was beautiful.

She'd been besotted with him.

She had enjoyed all of it up until the end—that was until he'd abandoned her. She'd not acted at all like an engaged woman. She'd acted like a trollop.

She and Mathew's nuptials had been hastily cancelled. Eliza's own parents had told her not to bother coming back home. If not for Thomas...

Her brother had welcomed Eliza back at the vicarage. She could assist him, he had reassured her, with cleaning and cooking and some of his paperwork. He'd taken her in unquestioningly despite adamant complaints from some of his parishioners.

The shunning she'd experienced over the next few years had been painful but well deserved.

"Would you care for some butter?"

Eliza snapped out of her musings enough to decline the plate Henry--Lord Crestwood-- offered.

"No thank you." Only in truth, the bread *was* dry, and she

would have appreciated a smidge of butter. But she didn't want to take anything from him. It was bad enough she was here.

She refused to meet his eyes.

"On second thought, I would." She took the plate before he could set it down. "Thank you," she added.

"How did the two of you meet, Father?" His son seemed willing to make conversation in order to relieve his boredom.

"While traveling."

"I worked at an inn."

They both spoke at once.

Oh, but he would wish to gloss it over for his children.

Lord Crestwood cleared his throat. "Ah, yes. The inn."

Heavy silence fell once again. After the maid cleared away the bowls, not even a minute passed before the younger man excused himself to follow her. The innkeeper's wife entered the room to refill their glasses of wine, and at the same time, Miss Fairchild excused herself as well.

Eliza would eat the last few spoonfuls that remained in her bowl and then retire for the evening. She had no wish to sit alone in Lord Crestwood's company any longer than necessary. She took a sip of wine and dabbed at her lips.

As the door closed behind the his daughter, Lord Crestwood cleared his throat a second time. "I am sorry."

Eliza did not look up at him, choosing instead to stare into her almost empty bowl. "That does nothing to change the facts." She didn't wish to dwell on this any more than necessary.

"I realize that." He'd raised one hand to his forehead. "But I cannot forgive myself, if that gives you any satisfaction at all."

"It—"

"And I know an apology means nothing. What I did… It was unforgivable."

"It was." Eliza finally forced herself to look up at him. "I never would have…" She could not bring herself to say the words. "I would not have!"

He stared back at her, and she required all her strength not to remember how gazing into his eyes had made her feel all those years ago. He'd always been so intense, and he was no different than that now. In fact, perhaps, he seemed even more so.

"It was unfair of me to take advantage of your innocence. My marriage made it even more deplorable."

Deplorable. Yes, an excellent description for what he'd done.

"Your daughter says your wife has passed." He was a widower now. "Are you remarried?" Why would she ask this? She did not care if he was married.

"She has." He nodded. "And I am not." It was his turn to stare down at the table.

"I'm sorry for your loss." She could not stop herself from uttering her condolences. It was what she did.

Even after he'd left her, she'd dreamt of his return. She'd wished… And he'd had a wife all that time.

"You never married," he commented.

"Brilliant observation." She half laughed. "No. I couldn't remain at the Dog and Pudding Pot after you left. After discovering us… Matthew wanted nothing to do with me. His mother wrote to my parents and they disowned me. If it weren't for my brother…" Why was she telling him all of this?

"The vicar."

"Yes. Thomas took pity on me. I've been with him ever since. I assist him with parish duties."

"So, your brother never married either. I remember you saying you thought he would marry once you moved out of the vicarage."

He'd remembered that?

"No, Thomas never married either." Oh, but she was

making them sound pathetic. "We are content though. It is a very satisfying life."

"Tending to the needs of others."

"Yes."

His returning stare seemed skeptical.

"It is," she persisted most adamantly.

"I am not arguing with you." His voice sounded languid again, now that they'd moved on from the subject of his horrific behavior. And hers… "I am only making conversation." He leaned back, folding his hands in front of his flat midsection. "Might I inquire as to where you are traveling to in the middle of winter? Some relative requiring caring for, perhaps? Seeing as you have become an angel of mercy."

Eliza stiffened her spine. "I have been invited to a house party for the holidays." She was not some charity case, nor was she a martyr.

At her words, his brows rose. "Indeed?"

"The Earl and Countess of Kingsley have invited me to their country estate, if you must know. The countess and I have known one another for several years. She grew up near Misty Brooke."

Upon this information, he shook his head and chuckled softly.

Eliza pinched her lips together. She hated that her gaze was drawn to the attractive creases that appeared at the corners of his eyes and that she wished he was laughing at some anecdote she'd recounted rather than the notion of her attending such an exclusive gathering.

"The countess is a dear friend of mine." She insisted.

Lord Crestwood grew serious. "The Dowager Countess of Kingsley is a distant cousin of my mother's. I only recently met the Kingsley's wife in London this past summer. Kingsley's estate is our destination as well."

He knew Lord *Kingsley's wife*? He had met *Olivia*? *Olivia* had invited Lord Crestwood to the same house party that she'd insisted Eliza attend?

Was it possible that her had friend done this on purpose? The year before, Eliza had told Olivia a rather innocent version of what had happened twelve years ago, while in the course of advising her not to carry on with the Earl of Kingsley—rather useless advice apparently—and she'd mentioned Henry's name.

Had Olivia remembered?

But that would be ridiculous.

Olivia could not have done this on purpose. He'd said they were family… simply an unfortunate coincidence.

Eliza inhaled deeply.

When the storm let up, she ought to return to the vicarage and write to Olivia that she'd changed her mind. She could not spend the holidays in the same house as this man!

The idea of returning home was appealing in some ways but quite disappointing in others. Eliza *had* been excited about the party. Something fun and different to break up the long winter months.

And what if Thomas had been anticipating the time to himself as well?

"You are traveling to Sky Manor as well?" She at least ought to verify the facts before making any decision.

"It seems we are to spend the holidays together." He lifted his glass of wine toward her. "Merry Christmas to us."

Eliza winced and ignored him.

With a shrug, he finished off his wine in one swallow.

Eliza closed her eyes. Nearly a fortnight in this man's company! Days on end with the constant reminder that she'd been complicit with him in committing the act of adultery.

How was she to endure it?

* * *

HENRY REMEMBERED why he'd been attracted to her in the first place. Not that she was the same as she'd been when they first met, but she posed such a contradiction of femininity, he found himself unable to abstain from teasing her—from goading her to speak her mind.

She sat across from him, stiff as a board, intent on proving to herself, to him, to anyone who cared to know her, that she rejected the needs most women had. That she was happy in her spinsterhood and felt no desire for anything more.

Guilt riddled his thoughts. She would have a great deal more if it had not been for him.

Vague memories flashed in his mind and forgotten emotions flooded in with them. Felicity had been incapacitated for two years at the time that he'd stumbled into that damn inn. He'd been in the depths of despair. His wife had been stolen from him, trapped in her own body. He'd never known such hopelessness and Eliza... He'd been drawn to her light. Her lure had been so innocent. And the passion. It had erased his pain for a time.

He'd never thought that he would do something so selfish. It was as though he'd wanted to fall in love again--go back in time--become a different person.

And he had. Somehow both his past and his future had disappeared over the course of that one week.

Had any of it been real? Had there been more between the two of them than physical attraction?

He disdained the thought as quickly as it came. She wanted nothing to do with him. She'd told him she hated him. She could never forgive him. And she had every right.

Besides, he was firmly established in his widowhood. His most pressing concerns were his children and the management of his estate.

"Your daughter is lovely. She resembles you a great deal." As soon as she spoke the words, however, she blushed, as though realizing she'd indicated he was lovely as well.

Henry would have chuckled but did not wish to add to her discomfort. "She was much easier as a child... These past few years, I feel as though I barely know her."

The woman across from him shrugged, and her shawl slid down her arm, revealing some of the skin along her nape and the slim line of her shoulder. "Five and ten is not an easy age for a young girl. Caught between being a child and a woman." Miss Cline's features softened at her words.

His daughter's moods baffled him. As much as he'd tried these past few years, everything he said to his daughter seemed either angered her or caused her to burst into tears. "It's as though we are speaking entirely different languages."

Henry's gaze landed on her hands as they drew her shawl around her shoulders once again. She was a tall, slim woman but not without a pleasant shape.

Miss Cline nodded. Her manner cordial... peaceful even, as she listened to his trials as a father.

She continued talking to him about some of the young girls in her brother's church, and he couldn't help thinking she would have made a wonderful mother.

His own wife had not been given much of a chance.

Bart had been little more than three and Charlotte not even two at the time of Francine's accident. She'd been so young. And after...

He shook his head, dismissing the painful memories.

"Anyhow, I wouldn't worry too much. She simply needs to find her way." Miss Cline smiled at him for the first time all day.

In fact, she smiled at him for the first time in twelve years. Ah, yes, he remembered why he'd been drawn to her before.

CHAPTER FIVE

CHANGE IN PLANS

Eliza hated that she dreamed of him that night. She'd done so almost nightly for the first year after he'd left, but eventually the dreams had tapered off, become less vivid.

Seeing him again had stirred them up. They were all too real sometimes, causing her to awaken with longings that disturbed her throughout the day. Causing her to wish…

She opened her eyes the next morning with that renewed sense of wanting. Rather than lie in bed in such a state, she quietly climbed out from the trundle and tiptoed to the window. She'd given up the larger bed so that Miss Fairchild would not have to sleep beside a stranger. She could sleep beside her maid.

The snow appeared to have let up, but large mounds of the white fluffy stuff covered the yard. Small flakes meandered from the sky but in the east, it looked as though the sun might perhaps break through and make an appearance later that day.

"Probably have to wait a few days to travel," Mrs. Blake spoke softly from across the room. "Hope the family doesn't have to miss the party altogether." She glanced surreptitiously toward Miss Fairchild, who snored evenly from the other side of the bed. "The children have not had an easy time of it."

Eliza wondered.

She would not ask Lord Crestwood about his wife but she could not help but be curious. "Lady Crestwood passed nearly a decade ago?" It was both a question and a statement. Ten years was a long time to mourn…

"No. But her ailment was rather morbid. Lord Crestwood had her cared for in a separate wing of the house, where the children would not be exposed to her… condition." Eliza blinked at the maid's startling words.

But… Miss Fairchild hadn't said her mother passed when she a child, but that she'd gone without a mother since then. Eliza raised her brows in question.

"Lady Crestwood didn't pass until last Christmas." The woman shook her head solemnly. "It was time, though. Poor dear. Never was the same after the accident."

Eliza's curiosity grew even more. At home, she'd done her best to avoid gossip whenever possible. As the vicar's sister, it had been her duty to set an example.

But she absolutely could not help herself. "When did she suffer her accident?" And what kind of accident? And why wasn't she the same afterward? But Eliza couldn't ask all these questions.

Mrs. Blakely twisted her mouth thoughtfully. "Hmm. That would have been… almost fourteen years ago, I'd say. Miss Fairchild was just a wee little thing." Realizing she might be revealing more of her employer than he might wish, Mrs. Blakely smoothed her skirt, reached for her apron, and turned away from Eliza. "I best be seeing about some chocolate for Miss Fairchild. If you'll excuse me."

Eliza nodded and then stared at the closed door for several minutes after the woman departed, confused, wondering what ought to feel. Were his actions even more unforgivable knowing that his wife had been at home, injured and infirm? Or were they less so?

Miss Fairchild moaned and rolled over in the bed, bringing Eliza's thoughts back to the present.

She dismissed her musings.

It changed nothing. He'd lied. Eliza took a deep breath. There was nothing to be done about it now. She glanced again at the snow-covered landscape outside the window. Lord Crestwood had made his choices, as had she. There was nowhere to go but forward. For now, however, she had another choice to make: was she going to miss the Christmas party in order to avoid him and his family?

Eliza missed Olivia. Her long-awaited time away from the vicarage stood in jeopardy. Likely, Thomas had counted on his time alone as well.

She would go ahead with her original plans. First, though, she must locate her driver. Coachman John, as he had told her to call him, had been sent by Olivia and Lord Kingsley so that she did not need to ride the mail coach. Although she'd written to her friend that the gesture would be far too extravagant, Olivia had insisted adamantly, giving Eliza no say in the matter.

She would find him this morning, however, so they might discuss when he wished to set out again.

Eliza dressed quickly, donned her shawl and climbed down the stairs. Stepping into the tap room, she found it more than a little curious to see him conversing intently with none other than the man who had been foremost in her mind for the past twelve hours, Lord Crestwood. They both appeared as though they'd already spent time out of doors, still wearing their coats and snow sticking to their boots.

Lord Crestwood glanced up first and grimaced at the sight of her.

Likely, he wondered if she would spew more hatred in his

direction. Shame washed over her but part of her remained adamant that he deserved every word she'd hurled the day before.

"Miss Cline." Coachman John seemed somewhat pained. "I've just been discussing the state of our coach with Lord Crestwood, here."

Eliza pinched her lips together. There had been that loud cracking sound when they'd pulled up in front of the inn yesterday. She'd hoped whatever was the matter would only require a quick repair.

"The futchel is broken all the way through and can't be repaired. I did some work on it yesterday, but until I can locate a replacement, that vehicle isn't safe." Eliza's heart sunk at the notion that she might be stranded in this inn over Christmas while the coachman went on to explain how this futchel piece connected some axletrees to splinter bars and other things she didn't understand.

"So, we cannot travel?" she finally interrupted him.

"I'm afraid not, Miss Cline." He truly looked disappointed himself. Of course, it meant he, too, would be away from his home over the Christmastide. And then he brightened somewhat. "Fortunately, Lord Crestwood here has offered us a ride to Sky Manor! I can retrieve the parts I need, and you can join Lady Kingsley's house party."

No wonder Henry had grimaced at the sight of her.

"I cannot impose—"

"It's no imposition. And my driver believes we can set out later this afternoon. We aren't far from Sky Manor and ought to be able to arrive before nightfall."

Could he not ask her opinion on these matters, rather than simply assume she would fall in line without question?

Only, it was rather generous of him, and he was also willing to help Coachman John.

She dipped her chin in acknowledgment.

"If we wait until just after the nuncheon, that ought to give the snow a chance to melt."

"I... Thank you." She lifted her gaze to meet his. And this time, at the sight of the lines around his eyes, and at the corners of his mouth, she contemplated the circumstances of his marriage. How ill had his wife been that he'd had to keep her away from her children?

Although he'd remained a robust-looking gentleman, his face seemed harsher, his eyes... haunted. How had she missed these details before? Was she only imagining them now?

"I've ordered breakfast." He seemed hesitant all of a sudden. "Would you care to join me?"

Ah, he was finally asking. A rumbling in her stomach reminded her that the soup she'd eaten the night before had not been as filling as she'd like.

"Thank you. Yes. I would."

He gestured toward the same private dining room they'd shared with his children the night before and, after the briefest moment of doubt, she preceded him inside.

* * *

HENRY HAD LAIN AWAKE, restless, most of the night, and it hadn't been because his son had been snoring loudly beside him. No, once he'd climbed into bed, memories of twelve years ago refused to allow him peace.

He'd been returning home to his wife and two small children after meeting with several physicians in London and being told in no uncertain terms that his wife's condition had no chance of improvment. They'd examined her several times already and told Henry he was wasting his time. His only course of action was to make provisions for the future.

He'd traveled the first day in a daze of hopelessness. He'd loved his wife when they married. He'd cherished her, in fact.

"Are you certain traveling today will be safe?" Miss Cline's voice jerked him out of his reverie.

Would it be safe? The sun slanted brightly across the small dining room. "If enough snow doesn't melt, we will delay."

Sitting across the table from him, he noticed that she wore a gown that was as dismal-looking as the one she'd worn the day before. Gray, with the same brown shawl wrapped around her shoulders. With her hair pulled back tightly, she ought to look austere, but instead, it drew attention to the classic perfection of her features.

Such a simple woman, and yet... Yesterday she'd breathed fire at him.

He deserved it.

"What happened to your wife?" Her question should not have surprised him.

Ah. What had happened to Francine? The question that had haunted his own soul for over a decade.

"She was attacked. On Bond Street."

Miss Cline blinked.

"We'd not been married five years. Bart was three and Charlotte had just turned one." Henry shook his head, still unable to comprehend the events of that day. In the past decade, his anger at himself had simmered into a deep self-loathing, for multiple reasons. "We were in London for the Season, and she'd gone shopping with some friends. A man..." he swallowed hard, "apparently wanted her reticule. Slammed her to the ground. She hit her head." The lump in his throat thickened his voice. "She didn't wake up for four days, and when she did..."

She'd invited him along that morning, but he'd declined, preferring to discuss some horses with a few fellows at White's.

"I should have been there to protect her. I was at my club."

She'd been unprotected, vulnerable.

Henry stared into the empty teacup before him. He'd not discussed these events with anyone in years. And yet…

The memory followed him from one day into the next, one year into the next…

"It left her in an altered state?" Miss Cline enquired in a sympathetic tone.

He pictured his beautiful wife, unable to eat on her own. Unable to speak but for a few garbled childish-sounding words. The unfocussed gaze her eyes had taken on. "You could say that." He hadn't meant his voice to come out sounding so angry. But it had made him angry.

All of it. Some physicians had offered false hope, and some had said she wouldn't live more than a month. In the end, they'd all been a little right and a little wrong.

Miss Cline nodded. "I'm so sorry."

What was she sorry for? He leaned back as a servant entered the room and then proceeded to pour hot tea into the cups set in front of each of them. Francine had been unable to ever enjoy hot tea again. After one attempt by her nurse, she'd burned her mouth and chin.

They'd been careful her food was never very warm from that day forward.

Miss Cline added cream but no sugar to her cup. Hers was chipped. His was not.

He drank his tea black.

"You say you just met Olivia, the countess, last spring?" Miss Cline was kind enough to change the subject. She could have delved into his tragic past; he supposed she had every right. But no, she would be sympathetic instead. "I haven't seen her since last March, since before she married the earl. She left Misty Brooke to have a Season with her sister and the next I heard, all of her belongings were being sent to Lord Kingsley's estate."

"Lady Kingsley is most enchanting," he offered. And she had

been. The family connection between Henry and Kingsley was a loose one. He had, in fact, been slightly surprised to receive the invitation. "I believe Lady and Lord Kingsley had only been married a month when I was lucky enough to become better acquainted with my cousin this summer. You mentioned that she is a friend of yours?"

Miss Cline nodded. "A very good one."

He felt some small relief to hear it. Henry imagined what Eliza's life had been like after he'd left her. After he'd ruined her.

"Was it horrible for you?" he surprised himself by asking. "After?" He wasn't sure if he was looking for reasons to feel better about what he'd done or more reasons to berate himself.

She paused with the cup just in front of her lips and tilted her head slightly. "It felt quite tragic, at first." She blew on the tea and then allowed herself a sip. She did not expand on her answer until she'd set the cup back in its saucer.

"Mathew's parents banished me from the inn, of course. Mrs. Wilson wrote to my mother and as a result, my parents told me not to bother returning home. But my brother has always been my defender. Thomas took me in and never made me feel as though he judged me for any of it, and he very well could have. When not a single person in the village would even speak to me, he provided me with protection and companionship, in addition to a place to belong, a purpose. He made it a point to preach often on the subject of forgiveness. On God's grace." She shrugged. "Eventually, people seemed to forget. It's difficult to turn one's nose up at a person who brings them a basket of preserves or turn someone away who is willing to help them in their time of need." She smiled sheepishly. "Matthew married a local girl the next summer. The two of them work with his mother at the inn." And then she raised her brows and twisted her lips. "Not so tragic, after all."

CHAPTER SIX

MORE THAN MEETS THE EYE

Eliza dropped her gaze and stared unfocused at her toast as she replayed her own words again in her mind. People *had* forgotten about the scandal she'd found herself in at the tender age of eight and ten. Even if they hadn't forgotten, they'd forgiven her.

Her brother had never once used her incident to belittle her.

And in truth, she hadn't missed Mathew as much as she ought to have. She had not been happy working at the inn whereas, her life at the vicarage was quite satisfying.

"I'm glad." Lord Crestwood sounded… relieved?

Eliza looked back up at him and blinked a few times. Not that what she'd done had been the wisest course of action to take, but what would she be, *who* would she be, if she'd married Mathew twelve years ago?

When Henry showed up in Misty Brooke, she'd been coming to realize Mathew and she had very little in common. Even before Henry had come along, she'd begun experiencing a myriad of doubts.

Had she truly loved Matthew, would another man have caught her attention so easily?

Which was no excuse at all, however…

Eliza appreciated that she could delve into a good book before bed. She enjoyed the fact that she could go visiting and help others when they were in need. If she'd married Matthew, she'd still be toiling under the watchful eye of Mrs. Wilson. She'd be raising her children with her mother-in-law questioning her every decision.

"I am sorry for saying… what I did. Yesterday. I only wish…" *That you had been honest with me from the beginning.* But did she? *That we had not taken that ultimate step of intimacy when it was wrong in every possible sense.*

But did she really?

Of course, she did! Her conscience warred with her wayward thoughts.

"It was inexcusable. I deserved it." He cleared his throat. "I returned home…" He cleared his throat a second time. "For what it's worth, it was the only time… Which, again, is not an excuse. Nor does it make my actions any less repulsive." There was no mistaking the disgust in which he viewed his actions. His voice was heavy with it.

She did not doubt his sincerity.

Eliza stared down at her lap. She supposed that it did matter. She felt a small stirring of respect to know he had not sought physical gratification with other women for the remainder of his marriage.

"And since her death?" She asked the question without thinking if it was an appropriate one or not. Not quite a year had passed. But surely…

"No one." He answered her, nonetheless.

For if his wife had been incapacitated, that meant he'd abstained for… Ever since the two of them had…

Not that other married men of the *ton* didn't practice infidelity regularly, but Eliza was a woman of God.

"It is worth something," she spoke the words quietly into her napkin.

Before either of them could say anything more, the door flew open and that younger version of Lord Crestwood came barreling into the room to take his seat beside his father.

"Good morning, Miss Cline, Father," he reached across the table for the jam as though he hadn't eaten in a week. "I'm positively starving. Are we leaving today? Do you think the roads will be passable?"

Conversation was led by Bartholomew Fairchild for the remainder of the meal until Eliza finally stood and excused herself. Both men rose politely and bowed in her direction.

"I'll be ready around one, then," she commented before slipping out the door.

She would be spending several hours in his company. His and his children's.

Had she forgiven him, then? The thought was a shocking one. Less than twenty-four hours ago, she'd believed him to be the cause of her fall into hell.

* * *

"I CANNOT SIT BACKWARD-FACING, Bart! You know that," Miss Fairchild grumbled at her brother, her backside protruding from the doorway of the elegant carriage that had been pulled around to the front of the inn.

"You cannot expect Miss Cline to ride backward. And I cannot either. Remember the last time...?" The siblings' argument carried out to the front porch of the inn.

Lord Crestwood was settling up with the innkeeper inside and Eliza felt hesitant to intrude. Nonetheless...

"I will ride facing the back," she said, interrupting the squabble in a firm tone.

Both of them peered out the door at her and spoke at the same time.

"That's not really necessary, Miss Cline, my sister—"

"My brother is more than willing to do the gentlemanly thing—"

"I would rather ride facing backward than have either of you get ill." Eliza smiled in as convincingly a manner as she could muster and then climbed in and made herself comfortable beside Mrs. Blake. Lord Crestwood would ride outside upon his mount.

"Have you visited Sky Manor before?" Eliza asked her traveling companions as they pulled out of the yard.

Bartholomew answered, "My father prefers we remain at his estate, Fair Lakes, when we're not at school."

"I'm dying to travel to London, but Father says it isn't safe. It's because Mother's attack, but he doesn't ever speak of it." Miss Fairchild glared at her maid's shushing before adding, "He's promised me a Season, however, as I've already mentioned, after I've turned seven and ten."

"Once he's established someone to sponsor you," Mrs. Blake inserted. "And he's only concerned for your wellbeing."

"Just because someone attacked Mother doesn't mean it's a common occurrence," Miss Fairchild argued.

"But look what it did to her," her brother rejoined.

"Did her assailant ever come to justice?" Despite all that happened, Eliza felt very sorry for the woman who'd been struck down at such a young age. It was difficult to imagine what that must have been like for the people who had loved her. She had been alive… and yet… From what she understood, she couldn't speak, or hear, or walk…

"A man was apprehended but Mother was unable to testify and since no other witnesses came forth, he was released. Our mother didn't recognize her own children, let alone a stranger," the son who'd lost his mother at far too young an age answered.

"Her brain was damaged." And then the young woman fell silent, as though unwanted emotions had crept up on her.

"She could do less than an infant," young Mr. Fairchild added solemnly. "But she was our mother."

"You two need to learn to curb your tongues." Mrs. Blake shook her head. "I would think those fancy schools would teach you what topics of conversation are inappropriate in polite company." And then, to Eliza, "My apologies, Miss Cline. We don't speak of the distasteful nature of Lady Crestwood's final years. God rest her soul."

Eliza blinked. "But she was their mother. I imagine it helps to speak of her." Eliza had sat with many of her brother's parishioners after they'd lost a loved one. She'd discovered the most soothing thing she could do was encourage them to speak of the deceased.

"Do you remember your mother at all, Mr. Fairchild?" she asked the young man sitting across from her. "Before the attack?"

"Call me Bart." He sent a sideways glance in his sister's direction." And my sister Charlotte."

Then he furrowed his brows. "I remember my mother a little. Moments, more than anything else. I do remember that she loved her garden. I remember playing in the dirt while she tended it."

"I have no memories of her from before," Miss Fairchild—Charlotte—piped in. "But Papa had a painting done. She looks normal enough in the painting."

"How difficult it must have been. To have her be present and alive, but her body and mind locked away from you."

Charlotte studied Eliza, seemingly considering her comment. "That's exactly what it felt like, Miss Cline. As though she was trapped in another world. That she could perhaps see outside of it but never allow us in."

"It wasn't so bad at first. I remember believing she'd get better eventually." Bartholomew removed his hat and ran his fingers around the brim. "But she only grew worse. I don't think she was trapped, so much, as gone altogether, leaving just the shell of her physical person."

"Doctors advised Lord Crestwood to send her away, but he never did." Mrs. Blake apparently had given up on discretion by this point.

"Sometimes she seemed angry and would thrash about. She hit me once, but I know she didn't know what she was doing," Bart defended his mother's actions.

"Of course, she could not have." Eliza couldn't help but suddenly feel great sympathy for what this family had endured.

And for Lady Crestwood, a woman who'd had everything, but then had her life ripped away in an instant.

"Lady Crestwood had less than a pound in her reticule that morning." This time, it was Mrs. Blake who was shaking her head. "Meaningless, so meaningless."

Eliza bit her lip. They were on their way to a Christmas house party, but one would not guess that if they took one look at the sad faces in their carriage. She decided to change the subject.

"Olivia… Lady Kingsley, that is, wrote to me that she and Lord Kingsley are of a mind to make this house party the best in all of England." This was only a slight exaggeration. Olivia's parents often had excluded her from their holiday celebrations and her new husband was determined to make up for it. "I wouldn't mind a little snow once we've arrived at Sky Manor. We could have snowball wars and make snow angels." She felt wistful all of a sudden, remembering one year when even her mother had played outside with her and Thomas. Their mother had been laughing and screaming when their father lifted her and then tossed her into a large drift of snow.

She hadn't seen them even once since that summer...

But she was no longer going to dwell on the past. She determined in that moment to embrace the festivities to come.

Mrs. Blake covered her mouth. "Oh, dear." The woman had turned a rather sickly shade of green.

"Stop!" Eliza pounded on the roof as hard as she could. "Driver! Stop!"

The coach came to a jarring halt, giving the maid just enough time to leap—with surprising ease—out of the carriage and dash to the side of the road. By the time Lord Crestwood turned around to see why they'd stopped, Eliza was at the woman's side and handing over her own handkerchief. Apparently, Mrs. Blake did not do well riding backward-facing either.

When all was said and done, it was decided that Bartholomew would ride Lord Crestwood's mount, Mrs. Blakely and Charlotte would ride on the front-facing bench, and Lord Crestwood would take the other half of the backward-facing bench.

Beside Eliza.

CHAPTER SEVEN

BESIDE HIM

It means nothing.

And yet all along her left side, Eliza felt a charge she'd not experienced in far too long.

God help her, but she was still attracted to him.

"Your coachman did well to stop so quickly," Eliza found herself babbling. "Otherwise, we might all have been covered in —" Good Lord! What was she saying? She clamped her mouth shut and just barely stopped herself from saying the word 'vomit' in his company.

Only he'd witnessed her doing the very same thing the day before.

It mattered not if she still found him attractive; chances of him reciprocating those feelings toward Eliza were slim to none.

She now realized that when he'd come through Misty Brooke all those years ago, he had very likely been in a deeply troubled state. He'd had two children who depended upon him and a wife who might as well have been dead but had been present every day to remind him of all that he'd lost.

He might as well have been attracted to a turnip. She'd been present and made herself… available.

Eliza pressed her knees together to keep her thighs from touching his. When the carriage began slipping, however, she couldn't help but slide directly into his person, pressing herself against the entire length of his side.

"I'm terribly sorry," she mumbled as they steadied, straining to remain upon her side of the bench. The snow, though mostly melted, had left this section of the road muddied and rutted. When they hit a particularly deep channel, she was all too aware that Lord Crestwood had set his arm around her shoulder. Mrs. Blake had done the same with Charlotte.

It meant nothing.

And yet she couldn't keep a shiver of awareness from running through her body. Could he feel it?

Another bounce and he held her even more tightly.

The driver slid a small overhead door open, allowing a ray of sunlight to slash inside and a cool breeze to swirl around the interior of the coach. "A bit tricky up here, M'lord," he hollered from outside. "I'll do my best but brace yourselves for a while. Pound on the ceiling again if anyone needs to stop."

"Very well, John." Lord Crestwood's answer was succinct.

Eliza ought to have been afraid they'd slide off the road, or that perhaps that the Furchel–thingymerbob would break on this particular carriage, but her senses were only aware of the man pressed up beside her.

Of the strength of his arm, the spicy leather aroma that laid siege to her senses. Without realizing it, she'd raised her right hand and grasped hold of the collar of his coat.

She felt his presence so acutely that she could have cried. *Get a hold of yourself, Eliza!*

The carriage creaked and groaned over the next half a mile or so, and then, just as quickly as the bouncing began, the ride turned smooth again.

Mrs. Blake released Charlotte and stared out the window. Charlotte rested her head on her maid's shoulder and closed her eyes.

Lord Crestwood did not remove his arm.

"It shouldn't be much farther." His voice vibrated beside her. She dared not look over at him for fear he'd read her thoughts somehow.

Fool that she was.

"Have you been to Sky Manor before?" Her voice sounded more breathy than normal. Hopefully, he'd chalk that up to the harrowing section of the drive they'd just endured.

"Once. Ages ago. But I know the area well."

She was all too aware of his hand resting on her arm. Beneath the wool of her coat and the cotton of her dress, she could feel the heat from his fingertips acutely. And she remembered in a flash how his hand had once felt upon her skin. She squirmed uncomfortably and he removed his arm.

But she no longer flattened herself against her side of the coach. She inhaled deeply to preserve the memory of his masculine scent. Her hand rested on her thigh and the length of her arm made the slightest contact with his.

And her heart raced.

"I imagine you're looking forward to becoming better acquainted with your cousins." She still did not look at him. Neither Mrs. Blake nor his daughter seemed at all interested in their conversation.

"I am. And you must be anticipating seeing your friend again."

"Indeed," she answered in lieu of anything more meaningful.

But what could they talk about in the presence of his daughter and her maid? "Do you think it will snow again?" she asked. Anything to take her mind off the most inconvenient turmoil that had sprung up inside of her.

He chuckled. Ah, yes. He knew. He knew precisely what she was doing. "It may." His voice held laughter. "Then again, it may not."

She could not help but laugh out loud herself. When she caught his eye, she saw something... interesting dancing there.

* * *

SHE WAS BREATHTAKING when she laughed. The thought struck Henry from out of nowhere.

Her eyes came to life, the corners of her mouth lifted, and her very essence tugged at something primitive inside of him.

"What's so funny?" his daughter demanded.

Henry tore his gaze away from Eliza Cline to instead settle upon his daughter. She oughtn't to be so shocked to hear him laugh.

Another thought that brought him up short. He hadn't done much laughing over the past few years. Come to think of it, his children hadn't either.

"I believe that I am simply relieved to have made it through that harrowing section," Miss Cline supplied. "Were you as terrified as I was?"

The thought that she had been terrified made him want to wrap his arm around her again. But of course, he could not. And she likely wouldn't have wanted him to.

Although, she hadn't seemed too reluctant a few moments ago. But then she'd squirmed as though she'd realized who was holding her and remembered how much she hated him. The thought was a sobering one.

"I wasn't afraid," Charlotte answered. His dear, brave daughter. Never wanting to admit to any weakness.

"I envy you, then." Miss Cline's voice still held a hint of laughter.

"One is unusually brave at such a young age," Mrs. Blake supplied.

Henry allowed his arm to relax, and in so doing, pressed it closer to the feminine one lying beside it.

She did not move hers away.

After he'd departed most abruptly from Misty Brooke, he'd done his best to forget the entire affair. In between bouts of guilt, however, he occasionally had remembered the emotional comfort he'd found with her. And that his body had enjoyed hers immensely.

They'd spent a good deal of time talking throughout the course of his visit—a visit he'd extended so that he could avoid returning to his wife and family.

He'd paid her silly compliments, and she'd delightfully flirted back. It was not until he'd taken her into the forest that night, to watch the woodpeckers hatch, that he'd crossed the line.

It had been her duty to make up his bed and clean his chamber. That last day she entered, and he'd closed the door behind her. She had known what he wanted. She'd not been shy or coy with him in any way. They both had seemed to want it.

He ought to have locked the door.

He ought never to have closed it.

Henry had barely found his release, bare-assed and quite satisfied, when the damn fiancé came barging in.

And by God, Henry had had the audacity to be annoyed with the man for barging in unannounced. The truth of the matter was that he'd been more angry with himself than anyone else.

Henry had not wanted to face the aftermath of what he'd done. The reality had been that he'd had nothing to offer her. He had no excuse for what he'd done, nor any explanation that could have satisfied her in any way. He'd not waited to speak with her. He'd not even left a note.

The fiancé had hurled all kinds of names at them both and then slammed out of the room. Eliza had been in tears, horrified by what she'd done. The memory was something he'd forgotten until now. But she'd kissed him on the lips before she'd dressed and gone after the other man.

She had kissed him... Why had he convinced himself that she'd gone to repair matters with the fiancé? To make him feel less horrible to abandon her? Henry replayed some of their conversations in his mind.

She had kissed him.

She had not been horrified to lose the fiancé. She had believed that he, that Henry, was going to offer for her. She'd believed Henry would protect her.

Rather than wait for her return, he'd paid his bill and departed in a hurry, determined to complete his journey home as he ought to have done initially. He'd vowed to love his wife, in sickness and in health. He'd vowed to forsake all others...

He'd left and done his best to pretend he'd not ruined the young woman who had trusted him. Or broken her heart.

No wonder Eliza hated him.

And yet, here she sat, in pleasant conversation with his daughter.

Was it possible he'd not ruined her life completely? Was it possible she was not dissembling when she'd asserted that she found her life satisfying?

Confounded, Henry only partly listened as Miss Cline managed to extract information about his daughter that Charlotte never would have shared had he been the person doing the asking.

And then his sweet daughter was laughing at some anecdote Miss Cline regaled about one of the boys in her brother's parish who'd gotten himself stuck in a large oak tree.

Henry's lungs filled and he felt... Was this contentment? The sensation was most unfamiliar. For the past decade, he'd gone through life carrying out his duties and responsibilities in what had felt like some sort of purgatory. For the past year, he'd finally been allowed to openly mourn his wife.

But that feeling… He inhaled deeply, hoping to capture it again. So foreign and yet he could not help but remember it from before…

"Oh, Father, is that it?" Charlotte asked with more enthusiasm than she'd shown him since she'd passed the age of twelve.

He glanced out the window and then nodded.

"If Crawford is here, it's possible he's brought his sisters, one of whom I'd guess is quite close to your age," Miss Cline offered.

"A duke's sister? Is she a pleasant girl?" The information had quite piqued Charlotte's interest in this house party.

"Oh, very. I only met her a few times, but they all seem like very sweet young ladies. Oh!" Miss Cline was peering out the window as well. "It's enormous! And so… majestic! I wonder how old it is."

This gave Henry an excuse to lean forward, to peer out the window from behind her and offer her some explanation.

"Lady Kingsley was telling me last summer that the main part of the house was built in the sixteenth century. Every fifty years or so, apparently, the lord of the manor adds a new wing. She told me it's very easy to get lost until one becomes familiar."

Miss Cline's lips parted in awe as she gazed out the window.

If he dipped his chin just a few inches, his lips would touch the delicate skin behind her ear. Already, soft tendrils of hair tickled his face. A lifetime had passed since he'd kissed her, since he'd inhaled her fragrance, and yet… he remembered. She must still use the same soap and wear the same perfume. She smelled sweet and clean, like snapdragons and sunshine.

He forced himself to lean back once again before his actions seemed untoward.

He had made her uncomfortable before. He'd best watch himself. He did not deserve to touch her. He could not flirt with her. He'd wreaked enough havoc already.

CHAPTER EIGHT

SKY MANOR

The carriage pulled to a halt and a uniformed footman approached and jerked the door open, sending a rush of cold air inside. Lord Crestwood exited quickly and then reached in to assist his daughter, Mrs. Blake, and then Eliza out and onto the ground.

Eliza chastised herself for enjoying the touch of his hand for that brief moment but didn't have time to dwell on her feelings. With a squeal of delight, Olivia came rushing down the wide stairs that spread out from the castle doors.

Because, yes, in truth, it was more castle than a house.

"Eliza!" Olivia shouted before rushing toward her and exuberantly embracing her in a warm hug. And if Eliza was not mistaken, her friend's belly seemed more swollen than normal. When they pulled back, she raised her brows in question and without her having to say a word, Olivia nodded, smiling.

Olivia had never looked happier.

"But why have you arrived with Lord Crestwood?" Olivia asked, looking far too smug for her own good. At that moment, Eliza knew her friend had remembered his name. She'd remembered the story Eliza had conveyed to her last year.

"Miss Cline, you are looking as beautiful and serene as ever." Olivia's husband, Lord Kingsley was magnanimous in his compliments, of course. Throughout his and Olivia's courtship, if that was what one could call it, Eliza had not withheld her disapproval. She blushed, a little embarrassed at her sanctimonious opinions.

This time, she sent him an approving smile. Because, indeed, his intentions had been honorable after all.

Lord Crestwood stepped up from behind her. "Kingsley." He grasped the earl's hand and then explained how they'd come across one another at the inn and how the coach they'd sent still required some repairs. After introductions between Olivia and Lord Crestwood's children had been made, everyone was climbing the stairs and chattering as they entered the cool foyer.

Eliza could not help but be awed by the magnificently high ceilings as well as the paintings hanging on the wall. Commanding suits of armor stood guard outside ornate doors that lined the corridor, sending a shiver of insignificance down her spine.

And for the first time, it really hit her; Olivia was a countess. And looking at her, not only was she a countess, but she was a woman in love, soon to become a mother.

Nobody deserved it more than her friend.

They'd driven for much of the afternoon and as the sun was nearly set, dinner was to be served shortly. A maid appeared, and Olivia instructed her to take Eliza to "the Rose Room." Everything seemed so luxurious. After traversing through several winding hallways, Eliza could hardly believe her fortune when she found herself in the most opulent chamber she'd ever seen. And to think it would be hers for her stay!

She would become spoiled for certain, and her little room at the vicarage would never feel the same.

When a knock sounded, she opened it to find a manservant

carrying her luggage and another maid announcing she was to attend to her for the course of her stay.

A lady's maid!

Eliza nearly laughed out loud. One look at the girl's face, however, and she knew it would have been unkind to do so.

She welcomed her inside and after the manservant left, found herself at odds with the reversal of fortune.

"My name is Sally. Shall I unpack your bags, then, mum? Her ladyship had me steam a few gowns before you arrived. She said your own dresses would likely need some airing out after your journey. If you'd like, we can order a bath brought up, but you haven't much time since the gong rang ten minutes ago."

That meant Eliza had all of fifty minutes to clean up. Even less so if she took into account the fifteen minutes required to make her way back to the main part of the house.

Had Sally said gowns? As in more tha none of them?

She turned and caught sight of a lovely emerald silk that the maid had pulled from the wardrobe. "This ought to look lovely with your coloring."

What had Olivia done? As her friend was at least six inches shorter than herself, Eliza knew these were not any of Olivia's castoffs. In fact, they looked to be brand new and suspiciously precise for her size.

What must it feel like to wear something so beautiful?

"I… um…" Eliza glanced around until she saw a washbasin. "A bath isn't necessary. Are you quite certain Lady Kingsley meant for me to wear that?"

Sally nodded her mob-capped head. She couldn't be much older than Charlotte. "There are silk slippers to match."

Eliza hadn't even realized she'd covered her mouth with her hand.

Oh, Olivia! What are you trying to do?

The gowns Eliza had folded neatly in her valise were not

much different than the one she wore now. Thick cottons in muted colors, dull with age and mended more than once.

The maid lifted the gown and held it in front of Eliza.

It was beautiful.

Before she knew what was happening, Sally was unfastening Eliza's gown from behind, lifting it over her head, and leaving Eliza standing in only her shift.

And for the first time in her life, Eliza Cline found herself being styled, pinned, and dressed by a most fashionably sensible ladies' maid.

Eliza didn't know whether to laugh or cry.

* * *

A SMALL BURDEN lifted off Henry's shoulders very soon after arriving.

Lady Kingsley had made a point to not only introduce Charlotte to the other young lady her age but had also gone so far as to place their chambers beside one another's. As easy as that, the young countess had given his daughter cause to look forward to the duration of their stay. Lady Martha, the youngest of the duke's sisters, was five and ten. Charlotte had been quite awestricken to meet the middle daughter and discover her to be nearly seven and ten.

And he'd realized that the young ladies, including his own daughter, were indeed that... *Ladies.* Not little girls. It was difficult to not think of this dark-haired emerging beauty as that same little girl who'd sat with him in Francine's room so many times. When he'd peeked into her chamber just now, she'd frowned at him for treating her like a child.

And she'd looked so very much like her mother.

"Stay out of trouble," he'd warned.

She'd responded with a groan. Would he ever cease to worry about his children?

He'd left the three young ladies giggling and pulling out dresses.

The older his daughter became, the less he seemed to understand her. He was only happy that Miss Cline and the countess had managed to crack her resistance somehow.

Once in his own chamber, he was pleased to find that his valet and thereby, his traveling coach, had not met with any difficulties and arrived intact. Not that he could not manage alone, but Martin had been in the family's service for decades. The gentlemen's gentleman would be devastated if not allowed to carry out the tasks of the trade he'd performed all his life.

And although halfway into his seventies, Martin exuded more energy than most fifty-year-old men.

"The dinner gong rang a while back, so we've not much time, M'Lord," Martin reached for Henry's jacket almost before the door had closed behind him.

Glancing around, Henry took stock of what was to be his chamber for nearly a fortnight.

Slanted ceilings, round windows, and odd angles reminded him that this was no ordinary home. And the large bed must have been built upon a pedestal of some sort, requiring a small set of steps to climb onto.

It was charming and for a moment, his breath caught. There it was again. Pleasure.

An odd sensation swept through him, and it took a moment to realize he anticipated the evening ahead. He hadn't anticipated much of anything for further back than he could recall.

He'd brought a valise full of work to do but only a small portion of it was urgent. He could make and attempt at enjoying himself, his children, his hosts, and the other guests.

Miss Cline.

Eliza.

Only he could not enjoy her in the sense he'd like. He'd

stolen her affection before and had no right to even attempt to… do what? Seduce her again? Woo her? Court her?

The irony of such thoughts was almost too much to bear.

He could, however, watch out for her. He could act as a protector of some sort, in the absence of her brother.

A handful of the other guests would be single gentlemen, and Miss Cline was likely not much more worldly than she had been twelve years ago.

He turned his head so Martin could shave the other half of his face.

Was it possible she could forgive him? He certainly didn't deserve it; he knew that much.

When she'd learned of his duplicity, she'd become physically ill. She'd flinched from his touch.

"I understand the countess has invited a number of available females, M'Lord." Of course, Martin would have no reticence in pointing something so personal out to Henry.

"And why should this be of any concern to me?" Henry attempted with a lift of his eyebrow.

Only Martin wasn't having it and merely laughed. "That Miss Cline, the lady from the inn, she's a pretty one, too, if one looks past her spectacles and fashion sense."

Henry took the towel from Martin's hand and dried his face. "Miss Cline is a fine woman."

Again, his valet laughed.

Henry merely shook his head. Difficult to stare down a servant who had saved you from more than one walloping when you were still in short pants. Smoothing the lapels of his jacket, Henry took one last look in the mirror.

And again, anticipation filled him.

CHAPTER NINE

ELIGIBLE BACHELORS AND UNMARRIED LADIES

Henry stared across the room at Lady Kingsley, who was snuggling her infant nephew against her shoulder. The new mama, the Duchess of Crawford, stood by with an adoring look on her face. It was rumored the newly married countess was with child herself.

"I've never seen Olivia so happy."

He turned around to nod in agreement but then froze.

He'd known Eliza was something of a beauty, with her perfectly classic features and expressive eyes but tonight…

Tonight, she looked stunning.

Dressed in a high-waisted emerald gown made of a material that gently embraced her curves, she took his breath away. Gone was the tight chignon knotted at the back of her head. Instead, her hair had been curled and pinned up. A few delicate tendrils had been left free to caress the curve of her cheek quite effectively, leading his gaze to her elegant shoulders and neck.

"Lady Kingsley," she added. "She's glowing."

But he could not drag his eyes away from the woman before him. "You… look different." Oh, hell, but he'd spent too much time away from civilized company.

At his comment, she self-consciously touched her hair and dropped her lashes as though suddenly uncertain of herself.

"No." He reached his hand out to pull hers back down. "You look beautiful." His eyes searched her face before trailing down to her décolletage. And lower. "Stunning."

"Olivia provided the gown. And the maid..." She stared down at the carpet.

And the realization hit him.

This woman had no understanding as to her beauty. And he wondered, was he to blame for this as well? It was only right he acknowledge the destruction he'd wrecked. And there was no atoning for it.

"It is perfect."

She lifted her lashes and met his gaze, uncertain but also with a bit of wonder.

"Miss Cline! I almost didn't recognize you without your spectacles." Neither had been aware of the duchess approaching to greet them. Henry had met Crawford's wife on a few occasions while in London last spring and found her to be a lovely woman in her own right. He made a deep bow.

"Your Grace." Miss Cline dropped into a curtsey. "The baby is beautiful."

The youthful duchess laughed in pleasure. "He looks just like his father. He's finally sleeping all night and that makes him even more beautiful to me, let me assure you." And then she took hold of Miss Cline's arm. "The boys are thrilled that they'll have an opportunity to see you. I hope you won't mind that I promised you'd be visiting the nursery. Michael was particularly excited."

Henry remembered hearing that the Duke and Duchess of Crawford had taken in a handful of urchins. Rumor was that the children had been left orphans after a tragedy that occurred on the duchess's father's property.

Miss Cline smiled graciously. "I do miss them, and I've

every intention of spending a good deal of my time with the children while I am here."

At his curious glance, the duchess provided some explanation. "His Grace and I have four other boys in addition to our little marquess. When the Smith children first lost their mother, and then their father, Miss Cline and my sister helped care for them before Crawford and I took them in." The duchess smiled. "They're a handful but every day we count our blessings. Our home is much happier with the laughter of children. And for the next few weeks, what with all the young people in residence, I imagine Sky Manor will be the happiest place on earth."

"It certainly will not be the quietest." But Miss Cline smiled kindly at the duchess.

As the vicar's sister, Miss Cline had obviously lived her adult life as something of an angel of mercy. Her natural ease with Charlotte made more sense to him now.

"Lord Crestwood has two children as well, only they aren't exactly children, are they? I believe his daughter is already becoming fast friends with Cora and Martha."

"My daughter is five and ten and my son nearly eight and ten," he provided vaguely, all the while watching Miss Cline deftly make conversation with one of England's highest-ranking women.

So very poised but also distant, almost as though it were she who was the duchess.

He wondered if she was ever lonely.

Two gentlemen approached just then and bowed. One he recognized immediately as the Duke of Crawford, and the other man was Mr. Gilbert Fellowes.

"Miss Cline. May I present Mr. Gilbert Fellowes? One of Kingsley's brothers." The duchess made the introduction.

Fellowes made his bow to Miss Cline, lifting her gloved hand nearly to his lips.

A pang of regret struck Henry. His cousin was a fine gentleman of good character. If she wished to have a family of her own, leave her brother's home, the earl's brother would be an excellent match for her. He stepped backward and then excused himself. Many house parties were prime husband-hunting grounds. He could not be part of the game.

Best to stay out of the crossfire.

* * *

HE'D CALLED HER BEAUTIFUL. Eliza's heart raced as she did her best to speak coherently to the duchess, her husband, and Mr. Fellowes.

Mr. Fellowes resembled his brother, the earl, a great deal but not in all ways. Both his hair and his eyes were lighter than the earl's. And he lacked the devil-may-care attitude his brother had exhibited while courting Olivia. His serious demeanor was calming. As she spoke with him, Lord Crestwood excused himself for other conversation.

"The countess has been singing your praises for as long as I've known her. As happy as she's been here at Sky Manor, I know she misses her sister and you a great deal." Mr. Fellowes' voice drew her attention away from the man across the room. Lord Crestwood had located the Dowager Countess of Kingsley, drawing a pleased smile from the older woman. Eliza had never been called beautiful by anyone.

Except him.

Before.

"Miss Cline?"

"Ah, yes, the sisters are quite close. I imagine they will remain so even though the countess no longer lives in Misty Brooke. It is not that long of a distance. A day's drive. Have you visited Crawford's estate, Ashton Acres?" Eliza did her best to keep her eyes focused on her present companion.

"I have not, but I now realize that perhaps I've been missing out on other delights to be found in the small village."

"Excuse me?" It took a moment for Mr. Fellowes' words to sink in. Did he mean her?

He smiled, and his light brown eyes held hers. "Indeed."

He was flirting with her! She scanned the room and found Olivia watching her with a gleam in her eyes. A slow smile spread across her friend's mouth as her hand cradled the head of her sister's infant son beneath her chin.

Eliza raised her brows in question, and Olivia dipped her chin ever so slightly.

The dress, the maid, Lord Crestwood. *Olivia had planned all of this.* She was providing Eliza with an opportunity to look for a husband, the matchmaking minx! Didn't she know that ladies such as herself, ladies close to their third decade, for heaven's sake, were not considered marriageable? Just as Eliza went to shake her head, Mr. Fellowes spoke again.

"My sister-in-law says you assist your brother with his parish. I find that most admirable."

Pleasure spread through her at the compliment. She did not go about her normal duties because her brother expected her to. She did so because it brought her genuine satisfaction. After a few weeks of wallowing in self-pity after Matthew had thrown her out and Henry had disappeared, she'd eventually realized that doing good for others made her feel… not deserving but not despicable either. She had discovered some self-respect again.

"I thank you, but there is nothing admirable about bringing myself pleasure." And with a furtive glance in Lord Crestwood's direction, she found herself wondering if he could had ever forgiven himself.

"It is admirable, nonetheless. You have nothing to drink. May I procure you something before we go into dinner?"

Mr. Fellowes, she realized at that moment, was quite a

good-looking man. And he seemed intent upon gaining her favor.

She smiled. "That would be lovely, thank you."

She was not left alone, however, as another of the earl's brothers, a younger man, approached with Olivia at his side. Olivia made introductions and then a few other gentlemen approached. Eliza nodded and smiled. Surely, all of this was Olivia's doing. She'd probably even asked her brothers-in-law to make certain her poor spinster friend did not feel left out.

But it was nice.

To be seen.

CHAPTER TEN

CONFUSING CORRIDORS

After the meal, a magnificent affair with more courses than Eliza deemed prudent, the ladies rose to return to the drawing-room, leaving the men alone to take their port.

As they strolled through the corridor, Olivia took hold of Eliza's arm from behind and pulled her close. "You can swallow your disapproval. I'll have you know that the food not consumed tonight will be made available for the servants." How well Olivia understood her.

Eliza chuckled. "It was the most delectable meal of my life," she conceded.

"And what of the gentlemen? I'm sure by now that you've guessed my ulterior motive for inviting you? Not that I am not simply pleased to have your company, but… do you find any of them to be… delectable?"

Lord Crestwood's face immediately came to mind.

Olivia leaned forward to look into Eliza's face as they walked. "You do! Is it Gilbert? Mr. Fellowes?"

Eliza clamped her mouth together. "Olivia, I am not discussing this." And then she added, "My Lady."

Olivia slapped her arm. "I am Olivia, and you are Eliza. I'll not have one of my best friends in the world my-ladying me."

Her dear friend had not changed at all.

Aside from being happier. And more confident.

Born with a crossed eye, Olivia had been self-conscious of it for as long as Eliza had known her. And Olivia's parents, the Viscount and Viscountess Hallowell, had exacerbated their daughter's apprehensions, making her shyer and more inhibited than what ought to have been natural for her.

Lord Kingsley had managed to squash the shame Olivia had cloaked herself in before. Eliza would be forever grateful to him for that.

"I'm too old to be thinking of any gentlemen as *delectable,*" Eliza said disdainfully, wishing she had not left her spectacles back in her chamber. When the maid had suggested she did so, Eliza had been so caught up by the dress, and her hair...

Foolish of her. Fancy dress or not, she was a spinster—a ruined one at that.

"Fiddlesticks!" Eliza did not have to turn her head to see that Olivia was scowling. "Is he the same as before? He is unmarried now."

Olivia had remembered! Of course, she was referring to Lord Crestwood. The fact that Olivia was now privy that Eliza's fling from the past had been with a married man was chilling.

The secret was not hers alone. Had Olivia guessed the extent of her ruin?

Glancing around to make certain no one could overhear them, Eliza felt the need to supply some explanation. "I did not know he was married!" she half-whispered. "And there is more to it than meets the eye."

Olivia stared at her in wide-eyed innocence. "I am no one to judge. And I am aware that his wife had been incapacitated. I merely wondered if the two of you...?"

"If we'd what?"

Olivia shrugged. "Still… found one another… interesting?"

"Shhh!" Eliza glanced around again, relieved to see that none of the other ladies seemed interested in their conversation.

"You do!" Olivia accused. It was impossible for Eliza to be angry with Olivia though. It was impossible for anyone to stay angry with her. She was just so… Olivia.

Eliza winced. "He lied to me. And then he…" Where had all of her outrage and anger gone? She could not blame him for seducing her. She had been an equal participant. Yes, he had lied. But as she'd just told Olivia, there had been extenuating circumstances…

"Too much has passed between the two of us for anything to ever…" Why was she even entertaining this conversation? "Mr. Fellowes seems like a kind enough gentleman."

She slid Olivia a sideways glance and found her friend studying her skeptically.

"Gilbert is indeed a man of good character. And if you've any doubt, I did not ask him to single you out. I have not asked anyone to do so."

"When did you begin reading my mind?"

Olivia squeezed Eliza's arm. "I always have. I just never let on about it…"

Eliza hadn't realized how much she'd missed her friend. Another lady who understood her so well. Before Olivia's marriage, she and Eliza had had a great deal in common. Neither had allowed themselves to consider any possibilities regarding marriage and family. They'd both resigned themselves to living out their lives as spinsters. But now that Olivia was entrenched in a loving marriage and soon motherhood…

Eliza was lonely. And for the first time in a dozen years, she wondered if she, too, might find some kind gentleman to settle down with.

The hope frightened her though. Disappointment was worse, sometimes, than not having any expectations to begin with.

Oh, but hope could be a lovely thing...

The drawing room transformed into a hive of activity as the other ladies milled about, some gathering around the pianoforte, others clustering into small groups.

As the hostess, Olivia was required to attend to all of her other guests, not just her oldest and dearest friend, and so Eliza excused her to her duties.

All of this talking and meeting new people was really quite exhausting! The socializing was so very different when done outside of her own little world.

Normally, she would have slipped outside, found refuge in Sky Manor's extensive gardens, but it was mid-December. She'd need to fetch her coat and a warm bonnet.

Would Olivia be offended if Eliza retired early?

With a hesitant glance around the room, she surmised that Olivia would likely be none the wiser.

Having made her decision, Eliza edged her way to the door and slipped out. She may have become more visible to a few of the gentlemen, but most of the other ladies still saw her as quite invisible. Not that anyone had been unkind or mean-spirited; quite the opposite, in fact. But she was not one of them; she was a vicar's sister. It was possible they expected her to begin quoting scripture if they deigned to start up a conversation with her.

If they only knew...

Out of sight, Eliza turned in the direction she believed her chamber to be and made her way determinedly through the castle.

At first, the adornments and corridors seemed quite familiar, but without her spectacles, she could not be certain. The farther she went, the less confident she became. And after turning back more than once only to find herself in unfamiliar surroundings, a vague panic set in.

She was lost.

She had thought she had climbed the same staircase she'd descended earlier. But... had she?

Taking a deep breath, she determined not to panic. She was quite safe; she'd only gotten herself turned around a few times. Catching sight of a window, she thought to calibrate her location by looking outside, but... It was so very dark already; she couldn't decide whether she was looking to the east or the west.

Another deep breath.

A few more unsuccessful attempts to discover more recognizable landmarks and panic swooped in on her again.

* * *

HENRY WOULD NOT SEEK Miss Cline out. He'd already decided upon this when the gentlemen, finished with their port now, strolled between the dining room and the drawing-room where the ladies awaited them.

She'd caught the attention of more than one very eligible gentleman already, and Henry would not do anything to ruin her prospects.

He'd already done his share of that. It only proved her kind-hearted nature that she deigned to treat him civilly. Nonetheless, when he stepped into the crowded room, his gaze immediately searched for the emerald of her gown.

Unable to locate her right off, he worked his way around various clusters of conversations so that he could assure himself that she was not overwhelmed or being made uncomfortable by any of the other guests—particularly the gentlemen.

He knew well enough that not all men of the *ton* always acted honorably.

By the time he'd covered the entire perimeter, he'd yet to have found her. Perhaps she'd gone to the retiring room?

He endured the company of one elderly gentleman, but when Lady Kingsley crossed over to present him to Lady Lillian, Crawford's oldest sister, he could not help but inquire as to where Miss Cline might have gone.

A curious expression crossed her face before she answered him. "She was here earlier. She might be tired from the travel today. I put her in the west tower of the Elizabethan wing." She lowered her brows in concern. "I do hope she didn't have difficulty locating her chamber. It's easy to get lost until one has become familiar."

And then she pursed her lips thoughtfully. "Perhaps I ought to send a servant to ensure she did not have trouble. Even with the sconces lit, these corridors are daunting after dark. I'd go after her myself if I wasn't required to remain with my other guests."

"If it would make you feel better, I'd be more than happy to take a look around that wing. It's near my own chamber, I believe." Of course, it was not the thing for an unmarried gentleman to go anywhere near a single lady's chamber, but if the countess was concerned...

She nodded thoughtfully. "Would you mind? I'd be ever so grateful."

"I do not mind at all." In fact, he'd feel better himself.

And so that was how he found himself wandering a literal maze of hallways fifteen minutes later. And it was a good thing he had, too.

For if he wasn't mistaken, the green he saw at the end of this particular corridor was the same hue as Miss Cline's dress. And the woman inside it looked more than a little distraught, huddled on the floor, her arms wrapped around her knees.

CHAPTER ELEVEN

A MISTAKE

After searching fruitlessly for her own chamber for all of half an hour, Eliza had not been able to suppress her panic any longer.

Tired, cold, and demoralized, she'd dropped to the floor and forced herself to breathe in and out in between a few pathetic, shuddering sobs.

"Miss Cline?"

Eliza lifted her forehead from her knees and tried to focus on the man in the distance. For the past ten minutes, she'd been doing her best to steady her breathing.

"Henry?" Surely, she was imagining it was him. But as he neared, she realized he was all too real. Even in the shadows and without her spectacles, she recognized his gait, his posture. *Him.* His pace increased as he neared and then dropped to his haunches in front of her.

"Are you all right? These blasted hallways go on forever." But his hands felt warm, rubbing along her upper arms in a soothing motion. "You're frozen through and through. Why didn't you find a servant to show you the way?" He sounded angry but his hands were gentle as he pulled her to her feet, up off of the cold floor.

She hadn't realized she was shaking. "I k-k-kept thinking I'd see something familiar around the next c-c-corner." This was so very foolish. To have become lost and then to have allowed herself to become so unnerved in such a dramatic fashion.

He removed his jacket, with a bit of a struggle, and placed it on her shoulders.

Overcome with relief, she buried her face on his shoulder, clinging to him as though he might run off and leave her alone again. When his arms wrapped around her, she relaxed only slightly and absorbed his warmth. "S-s-stupid of me. I'm so sorry."

But his hands soothed up and down her back now, and he was whispering reassuring words. "It's all right. Anyone could get lost in these halls. No need to be sorry, my dear. I'm only relieved that I found you."

Oh, but he smelled safe and comforting.

It reminded her of how she'd felt before. How she'd wanted only his protection and love.

The desire to push him away warred with the part of her that had… missed this.

Missed this dreadfully.

Her hands rested on his chest, and she could feel his hard length from the top of her head to just above her knees. *Henry.* She wanted more from him, just as she had all those years ago.

"Lady Kingsley was worried that you might get lost. Allow me to escort you to your chamber and then I'll go assure her of your safety." His voice sounded gruffer than it had before.

Olivia had asked him to come after her! But of course!

Eliza was going to have to have a serious talk with that young lady. For a few glorious moments, Eliza had thought he might have noticed her absence and come after her out of his own concern.

She swallowed hard and forced herself to step out of his arms. "I'm sorry you're missing out on the evening's entertainments." Although she had no idea if there were any, other than the conversation and excitement of the first night of a house party. "It was foolish of me to attempt to locate my chamber on my own."

He'd dropped his hands when she'd stepped away but otherwise had not moved. His green eyes seemed as though he wanted to say something to her, but she was very good at imagining such things—especially where Henry Fairchild, Lord Crestwood, was concerned.

"A mistake. We all make mistakes." And when her gaze met his, he smiled sadly.

Something unrecognizable squeezed her heart.

"I do not hate you." The words rushed past her lips. "It was a mistake. But we are all human, are we not?" And then she added again, in a most resigned-sounding whisper, "I do not hate you, Henry."

A light flickered behind his eyes but disappeared just as quickly. "You are too kind." He scrubbed a hand down his face. "My wife was injured—slowly dying. And I…"

"Made a mistake," Eliza filled in for him.

Again, he met her eyes and nodded.

Eliza bit her lip. "So…" She glanced up and down the dimly lit corridor. "Do you have any idea where we are? If we can make it back to the main foyer, I can ask a maid—"

"Lady Kingsley told me the location of your chamber. I believe I can get us both there as mine is in the same vicinity." He winged an arm. "Shall we?"

Eliza swallowed around the sudden lump that seemed to have lodged itself in her throat and then placed her hand in the crick of his elbow. It was almost bittersweet, to touch him again, the same as any lady might do when presented with the polite gesture.

At first, she thought they were walking in circles again and yet she felt none of the fear that had gripped her earlier.

He made her feel safe.

And then they climbed a spiral staircase and the painting she'd taken note of when she'd first arrived appeared before them. "Right here," she said, almost in awe. By now she'd been lost for nearly an hour.

He halted but did not release her immediately. He gestured across the hall. "My chamber is right here. If you have need of going anywhere—or have need of anything—don't hesitate to come to me."

He would be sleeping only a few dozen feet away from her, separated by a hallway, walls, and two heavy doors, of course, but still…

She nodded. "You will tell Olivia, the countess? I hate for her to worry."

He looked tired but nodded. "I'll locate her directly. It's been a long day. I'll check in on Charlotte and Henry and then retire, myself." He paused, again looking as though he had something more to say. "You are quite certain you are all right?"

She nodded again and shrugged out of his jacket for the second time in as many days.

"And you'll… come to me if you are not?" He took the jacket slowly, making her imagine he wished to delay their parting.

She searched his eyes, wondering what he was thinking. "I will."

Realizing he was not going to leave until she was safely inside her chamber, she opened the door behind her and backed into the room. "Thank you. I don't know what I would have done…"

"You never have to thank me for anything." A gravelly tone sounded in his voice. Holding the jacket in one hand, he bowed sharply.

She stepped all the way inside and closed the door.

She wanted him. God help her, but she wanted him.

She turned, pressed her back against the door, and closed her eyes. She was a vicar's sister—a Godly woman. And yet, she would not allow herself to have the dreams of him she'd had as a young girl. Dreams that had involved an offer of marriage, a lifetime of loving, of sharing and caring for a family together.

He'd not indicated the desire for any of these things. Even if she thought he did, she could not trust herself.

But she wanted him.

* * *

HE WANTED HER.

Henry tossed his jacket onto a nearby chair and then rubbed the muscles at the back of his neck.

Even after locating Lady Kingsley and informing her that her friend had been safely delivered to her chamber, checking in on his daughter who had made arrangements to share her chamber with Lady Martha, and ascertaining that Bartholomew was keeping out of trouble, he could not shake the need Eliza had ignited.

He had grown surprisingly adept at resisting temptation. The guilt he'd experienced twelve years ago had been enough to curtail any further deplorable behavior on his part. Even now, with Francine buried in the small cemetery on the edge of his estate, he found himself hesitant to seek any sort of physical gratification with a woman.

For twelve long years, he'd made do with finding his own release and now… Hell and damnation, any other man would think he was bent for Bedlam.

He was not worthy of her.

Of any decent woman.

CHAPTER TWELVE

A FLICKERING SMILE

After spending two full days indoors, Olivia declared that despite the cold weather, they must explore the magnificent landscaping of the gardens at Sky Manor. Most of the plants were dormant but there were follies and paths and vistas that all begged exploring, nonetheless.

A few of the older guests declined, but nearly everyone under the age of forty was game.

And the minute she stepped outside, Eliza decided it was, indeed, a brilliant idea.

The combination of crisp air and sunshine was exactly what everyone needed. It also gave her an opportunity to wear the lovely cloak that had shown up in her wardrobe, red velvet with a white fur-trimmed hood.

"Almost all of the snow has melted." Lord Crestwood stepped up behind her. She did not need to look over her shoulder to know it was him. She'd noticed that she could practically feel the air change whenever he was near.

"It's a beautiful day, though, don't you think?" She turned to gage his reaction.

A smile flickered on his lips. "It is." And then he pointed to a small structure in the distance at the top of an imposing hill. "Are you up to the climb? I do believe that the peak is Lady Kingsley's destination for us all."

"It's practically a mountain." But Eliza stepped forward eagerly. She'd enjoy his company for now. She was not mistaken, he'd avoided her since the evening of their arrival. Although he was never too far away…

"Tell me about your home. I know so little about you," she urged him.

She knew the major events that had defined his life for the last decade and a half, but she didn't know anything about his likes, his hobbies. What made him happy.

As the path was wide here, he walked beside her, both hands behind his back. She could not help but think that despite wearing what looked to be a well-worn, favorite jacket and waistcoat, he looked very lordly and very distinguished. Rather in the manner in which he held his head, the set of his chiseled jaw.

"Fair Lakes is in the south, about ten miles from the sea."

"And you are the baron." She slid him a sideways glance. "Not the second son." As he'd told her when they first met. But she spoke the words with a gentle smile.

He nodded. "Ah, yes. What other lies did I tell you back then?"

"That you'd been on a leisurely journey. I take it that was a fabrication."

They walked several yards in silence, the climb becoming gradually steeper. The youngsters had taken off and were now far ahead of them and Olivia and her sister trailed behind with other guests.

"I had gone to London to meet with a group of physicians. They'd all examined Francine at one point and had conferred over her case. None of them were able to offer any hope for her condition."

"You loved her." This was not a question.

"I did. By the time I met you, she'd been in her disoriented state for two years. It was as though her physical body was there but not her spirit. Not her person."

Eliza could not imagine going through that with anyone, let alone a spouse.

"And so you were... distraught when we first met."

Again, they walked several steps with no words exchanged.

"I was numb. When I met you, I wanted to be somebody else. It doesn't make sense, but I offer no excuses, I simply... acted poorly."

He slipped behind her as the trail narrowed. And when she stumbled slightly, he grasped her, only for a moment, by the waist.

"You seemed happy." This was something she didn't completely understand. "I suspected nothing." She wished she could see his face but had to concentrate on the ground ahead.

"When I met you, I felt... almost drunk. You were young and innocent. I'll not deny that I found you incredibly attractive. If I hadn't been a married man..."

Eliza swallowed hard. It was still difficult to acknowledge what she'd done.

"We cannot change the past. We can only paint our futures." Only he had far more choices in painting his, as a man, a titled man at that, than she did. A woman of the lower classes was not presented with many opportunities.

She had been young, eight and ten, when they'd first met. He'd been an older gentleman and he'd found her attractive. And now? Twelve years later... Women were on the shelf by the age of five and twenty and yet an eligible man was eligible... Good heavens! Until he was buried six feet under.

She might as well be in her dotage. Be that as it may…

But she had daily choices. Opportunities to offer comfort, to improve the circumstances—even if only slightly—of those around her, of those less fortunate.

She had the opportunity to draw a smile from someone who had little reason to smile.

"We can make every day a little bit like Christmas, if we so choose." She observed.

Eliza selected that moment to pause in her hiking, her breathing somewhat labored as she hadn't slowed her pace with the steeper grade.

Lord Crestwood stopped as well and seemed to be studying her. "You are an impressive person, Miss Cline."

"I am not."

"No. Do not deny me this compliment."

She backed up against a nearby tree and leaned against it, feeling almost feminine—almost pretty, and not only because of the elegant cloak Olivia had provided.

But because of a man.

This man.

Those following had fallen out of view and she could no longer hear the chattering of the group ahead.

"Very well." She could almost remember how she'd flirted before. "I will not deny you."

She was on holiday. He was no longer married. Was she so very foolish to want for him to kiss her?

He stepped forward, causing her heart to jump, but then seemed to catch himself. He cleared his throat and then skimmed his gaze over everything but her.

Oh, but she was foolish! Did she not remember that she'd been invisible before coming here and wearing Olivia's fine dresses? Did she not remember that she was nearly thirty? That she wore spectacles and was an uninteresting spinster?

He must think her quite forward and somewhat pathetic.

She pulled herself away from the tree and pushed onward. Thank heavens he was behind her so that he did not see the tears she refused to allow to fall.

* * *

HE'D ALMOST KISSED HER.

Henry followed closely in case she stumbled on one of the tree roots that grew across the path, all too conscious of her derrière swinging naturally with each step.

She wanted him to kiss her, he was certain of that. Just as she had before. When he'd taken advantage of her.

His guilt would not allow it this time.

Even if he was no longer married, and she was no longer a naïve girl who was engaged to the Inn owners' son.

He hated himself whenever he remembered it. And yet. It was not fair to her for him to regret what they'd done. She slowed and lifted her skirts a few inches in order to pick her way around some rocks. He could not keep from smiling at the sight of her most practical boots.

Such a contradiction of femininity.

One minute fluttering her lashes at him, her lips parted for his kiss, and the next marching sternly toward the top of a mountain.

Why can't I kiss her?

What had she said?

We cannot change the past. We can only paint our futures.

"If you could change the past, would you?" Perhaps this was an obnoxious question to ask her. Good Lord, she'd become physically ill at the sight of him less than a week ago. Of course, she would change it.

"What we did was wrong," she huffed.

So, she would. She would wipe her soul clean of their sinful affair.

"But I would not." And then they turned the corner to a view that stretched for miles as well as a buzzing group of boys and girls on the cusp of adulthood.

"What took you so long?" Bartholomew teased them. "We've been here for hours."

CHAPTER THIRTEEN

AN UNEXPECTED GUEST

A low murmur of conversation hummed in the room. It was late in the afternoon but not so late that everyone had returned to their chambers to dress for dinner.

But Henry was not interested in any of the discussions nearby. And on this afternoon, the day before Christmas Eve, he was only curious as to the conversation between Miss Eliza Cline and his son, taking place near the large terrace doors.

Bart stood earnestly nodding and then cast his gaze downward as Miss Cline placed one hand upon his son's shoulder. *What on earth?*

Henry edged closer, wishing he could somehow make out their words. Before he could join them, his unruly son brushed his hair back from his forehead and nodded solemnly at her, bowed, and then slipped out the French door.

Living in the same house with her over these past few days, watching her with friends and people who treated her almost like family, Henry realized that he'd only ever known one aspect of this woman.

Without fail, if assistance of any kind was ever needed, Miss Cline was the first to come forth. If the children required attention, she did not hesitate to provide it. If one of the countess's elderly guests was left alone, Miss Cline sat down to chat with them.

Lady Kingsley had quite adamantly declared that the children were welcome to join in the festivities along with the adults. Christmas was not very merry without the laughter of children. The adults, she insisted, had the evening meals and later to themselves.

And so he'd spent more time than usual with his own offspring. It had been… enlightening.

A few times he'd found Miss Cline in conversation with his daughter and Lady Martha, offering suggestions for the young women to entertain themselves so they did not end up wallowing in their chambers. Charlotte had seemed to shed the sullen behavior he'd become accustomed to.

And if he knew his son, Henry had some inkling as to the topic that curious conversation had entailed.

As though sensing his stare, Miss Cline pushed her spectacles up the bridge of her nose before glancing over to catch his gaze.

The two of them had not spoken privately since they'd hiked up to the folly together. Oddly enough, however, he constantly seemed to know where she was, what she was doing, and who she was doing it with.

She approached and then dipped into a delicate curtsey. "Lord Crestwood. You are enjoying the house party, I hope?" A flush of enjoyment tinged her face a pretty pink and her brown eyes shone warmly from behind her spectacles. This woman, he was coming to realize, was happiest when she was going out of her way for others.

A giver.

"Immensely."

Yes, almost every other person saw this woman for her

deeds. They saw her efficiency, her dedication, and sense of duty.

"And you?" he asked. "Are you enjoying this time away from the vicarage?"

There was so much more to her. He'd known her as a woman—a woman of passion. And still. He recognized a… wanting in her. He was fairly certain those passions still burned just beneath the surface. Or perhaps deeper.

He wondered who she would allow to ignite them once again. For she would allow some fellow into her life, into her bed.

She was not satisfied with her present circumstances. He was certain of it. He'd be surprised, in fact, if she departed from this house party without accepting an offer from Kingsley's brother, Joseph Fellowes.

Mr. Fellowes seemed quite taken with her and… he would make a fine husband, but…

Henry bristled at the thought.

She smiled brightly. "The young people are excited for tomorrow. If only the snow would return." And then she laughed. "I shall not be greedy. If it does not snow, that simply means we will have an easier time collecting the greenery."

"You are the least greedy person of my acquaintance." And he meant it. But some devil inside of him had him thinking that she'd been greedy in bed.

And good God but he was a cad for remembering.

He'd touched her intimately. He'd come to remember more and more of time spent with her long ago. Lying in his bed, knowing she was so nearby, he'd remembered.

Before their tryst had come to its abrupt ending. Soft tender lips had been eager to taste him. She' had been eager to learn the secrets of passion.

That was all he'd been able to give her then.

But legally, now, he was free to marry—if he so pleased.

He swallowed hard. Did he? Did he want to marry again?

"You have managed to succeed with my children where I've found little success."

She tilted her head, confused.

"They listen to you." He'd noticed. "They talk to you." He clamped his lips together, irritated with himself on these points. "Will you tell me if my son is up to no good?"

"They look up to you a great deal; it is just that you are their father." She winced. "Without breaking Bart's confidence, I will tell you that it appeared he might be moving in that direction, but, apparently of mind to heed some carefully given advice, I believe he has realized the error of his ways."

Henry met her gaze steadily and then cocked one eyebrow. "That pretty little maid who has been lurking around him all week?"

Miss Cline bit her lip. "I promised I would not say. However, be assured that he has been apprised as to exactly what sort of man takes advantage of ladies who are in service." Henry reeled back at her words. "I did not mean—"

His heart skipped a beat at the unintended insult. Not that he did not deserve it, but her kindness had made him think she'd forgiven him. She had told him she did not hate him. And she may even have meant it. But he'd extrapolated far too much from that. He had hoped…

Henry stepped away. "You are right though. I appreciate your setting him straight on such a matter. And I also thank you for not holding his father up as an example."

He was frustrated that he could do nothing to change the past, to atone for his actions. The dye had been permanently cast, painting their association tarnished for all time. Damned fool that he was, he'd watched her because he… liked her. And he'd wondered…

Perhaps he would forgo dinner. Perhaps he ought to forgo the holidays completely.

If he weren't a father, if two young people did not depend upon him... He'd what? At times he felt he was only a shell of a person. But he was needed.

And although his children didn't show it most of the time, he knew that he was loved.

* * *

She realized what he would think the second those ill-advised words left her mouth. She had been a servant, of sorts, when they'd met before. He'd think she was directing her insult at him.

But she had not!

All week long, she'd been acutely aware of his presence; his steady calm, his gentle demeanor and patience. And no one could fail to see the love he obviously felt for his two children—despite their youthful angst. She knew he'd borrowed Lord Kingsley's study on a few occasions to finish some estate correspondence and that he rode early each morning with a few of the other gentlemen. At times, he seemed as though he were simply going through the motions of fatherhood, of life.

And yet she knew that he tried. And for that, Charlotte and Bartholomew would one day see how lucky they were to have such a man for a father.

Of all things, she didn't want for him to believe she thought poorly of him.

Quite the opposite, in fact.

She reached out to touch his arm, to correct the assumption he'd obviously made, but before she could speak, the drawing-room doors flew open and of all men, her brother came storming in. He wore one of his older suits, his cleric collar, and a scowl deeper than the one he showed while delivering his most fiery of sermons.

"Vicar Cline?" Olivia stepped forward. "You decided to join the house party after all?"

"Thomas?" Eliza stepped away from Lord Crestwood. She could hardly believe her eyes. Not only at her brother's presence but at the rage emanating from him.

Her brother was a quiet man, a kind and gentle one.

His gaze pinpointed her in accusation, and he charged across the room, grasping her arm almost violently. He did not appear as though he'd come to take part in Olivia's holiday entertainments. He looked determined.

Determined and furious.

"What are you doing here?" She attempted to pull him away. Somehow, she feared that whatever he had to say was not going to be appropriate in mixed company. But he resisted her.

"The question, Eliza, is what you are doing here?" His jaw set grimly. "Mrs. Frye received a letter from one of Lady Kingsley's guests. The concerned woman felt it her duty to make it known to one of her *dearest friends* that *he* was here. Why would you remain, Eliza?" Her brother stared at her in confusion, but she saw hurt in his expression as well. "I had thought you were smarter than this! After everything..."

He?

Did he mean Lord Crestwood? She opened her mouth to answer but before any words emerged, Thomas cut her off. He lowered his voice but it came out sounding almost like a snarl.

"Do you think I did not know his identity? Of course, I did! Everyone did! It was a long time ago, and people forgive, but they never forget. If word gets out about this, and you do not return home immediately, I'm not certain Misty Brooke will be so forgiving a second time."

She had thought no one cared about it anymore.

She had believed she'd been forgiven. Had she been naïve in thinking she'd paid her penance already? "Thomas..." she began again.

"Cline." Henry stepped forward from behind her, one hand outstretched toward her brother. "I believe I am the person to address regarding this matter."

But Thomas only scowled deeper, narrowing his eyes.

Oh, no! This wasn't happening! Not at Olivia's party!

At a loss as to what she could say, Eliza's upbringing and manners took over. "Lord Crestwood, I'd like to present to you my brother, Vicar Cline. Thomas, this is Henry Fairchild, Baron Crestwood."

Her brother obviously recognized the name immediately. He said he had known all along. He said that everyone had. Not once had he asked any of the details when she'd gone to him after the Watsons ordered her to leave.

But Thomas had indeed, known the culprit of her ruin.

Of course, Mrs. Frye had gone to him right away. Eliza wondered fleetingly which of Olivia's guests had written to Misty Brooke's most efficient gossip.

"You may be a nob, but that doesn't mean you can simply take whatever you wish, whenever you wish it. How dare you even lay eyes upon my sister? After what you did? If I wasn't a man of God, I'd—"

Eliza cringed at her brother's words. *Oh, Thomas, no!*

He was here to protect her, to save her--from Henry Fairchild!

"Why don't the three of us move this to my study." Lord Kingsley stepped between the two men. "Not well done to interrupt my wife's party, wouldn't you agree?" Beneath the earl's affable charm, Eliza heard an edge of steel.

She didn't believe she'd ever seen the earl angry.

Eliza ought not to have come. As soon as she realized Henry would be here, she ought to have returned to Misty Brooke and spent the holidays at home. Why had she not considered this? Having their names linked together in any way, whatsoever, was only going to provide fodder for the gossips.

How naïve she'd been to assume the people in her brother's parish had forgotten. She'd thought she had atoned for her sins. She'd thought she'd become one of them.

"Apparently, you know nothing of the kind of man you've welcomed into your home." Her brother turned on the earl, his face red with rage. How could he speak thusly to Lord Kingsley?

Eliza stepped forward and took her brother by the arm. She needed to stop this before he went too far.

He shook her off, and Lord Crestwood stepped forward.

This was getting out of hand quickly. Thomas had obviously spent the entire journey between Misty Brooke and Sky Manor summoning all his might to avenge her.

"Thomas, please. Not here." Eliza glanced over her shoulder. Of course, all eyes were upon them.

"Mr. Cline, I would request a word with you alone." Lord Crestwood spoke in a calm but firm voice.

"The only word I'll have with you is on a field of honor." Eliza had never seen her brother so worked up. She could not allow him to go on this way, most definitely not in her defense.

"Thomas! No!" She went to step forward again, but this time, it was Lord Crestwood who took hold of her arm. Gently though, and in a reassuring manner.

"By God, get your hands off her—" Thomas went to lunge, but Lord Kingsley and the Duke of Crawford held him back.

And then, in a calm and matter-of-fact voice, Lord Crestwood spoke perhaps, the only words that could subdue her brother's attack: "Your sister has consented to marry me."

The words, in fact, silenced the entire room.

Eliza stiffened beside him. He thought that he had to do this. But he did not! She did not want a man, even this man, to marry her out of obligation or guilt. All that was required right now was to get her brother away from Olivia's guests. "But—"

"So, if you don't mind," Lord Crestwood smoothly interrupted her to continue addressing Thomas, "I think we ought to take Lord Kingsley up on his kind offer and move this discussion to a more appropriate setting."

At that moment, Eliza would have gladly returned to being the invisible lady she'd considered herself. Finding herself the center of attention, the object of all eyes in a room, was not a comfortable circumstance by any means.

Thomas blinked a few times, removed his hat, and finally turned to look at Eliza again. "Is this true, Eliza? He has offered for you?"

Lord Crestwood squeezed her arm gently. He stood close enough beside her that she could almost feel him holding his breath.

"I–um." She glanced sideways at him with questioning eyes. *He does not have to do this.* He was only doing it out of guilt. He didn't love her.

And yet... his warmth at her side and back comforted her. She could not help remembering how it had felt to be held in his arms.

She should deny it. She should end this now.

"Yes." She exhaled. "It is true."

CHAPTER FOURTEEN

BETROTHED?

As quickly as Thomas had arrived, Lord Kingsley, the Duke of Crawford, Lord Crestwood, and Thomas all excused themselves to disappear, presumably, into the earl's study. When Eliza went to follow, Olivia took hold of her shoulders from behind and ushered her away from the large drawing room and into another, smaller sitting area.

Eliza wrapped her arms around herself. She had not realized that she was shivering. "I'm so sorry, Olivia."

Olivia steered her to a loveseat and dropped a shawl over Eliza's shoulders, all the while shushing her apology. "If anyone is to blame it is Mrs. Frye! Benighted gossip! You, my dear friend, have nothing to apologize for. Absolutely nothing."

"But… such a horrid scene! Your wonderful Christmas party. I wanted it to be perfect for you!"

Olivia laughed. "You should know as well as anyone that to expect perfection only invites calamity. Let's forget about the party for now. I'm dying to know! When did Lord Crestwood propose? I had so hoped the two of you would fall in love again. He's simply the most delightful man, aside from Gabriel, that is, and he's been through so much. When I met him last summer, I just knew you had to see him again."

Eliza laughed and at the same time, a choked sob escaped. "Oh, Olivia. Not all of us can be as lucky as you and your sister have been." She gulped down another sob. "Don't you understand? He has not proposed! He only said he did in order to subdue Thomas. And now… I'm going to have to tell Thomas the truth, and all of your guests will know that I lied—"

"Why is it impossible for you to have the same sort of luck? I've watched Lord Crestwood this week. And he has been watching you. At first with a curious sort of expression, but as the days have passed, I have seen longing in his eyes."

"You are imagining things, Olivia."

But Olivia was shaking her head. "You are one of my dearest friends but also one of the most pessimistic women of my acquaintance. You were wrong about Gabriel, and you are wrong about Lord Crestwood. Just you wait and see."

Eliza merely shook her head. Although she had been very wrong about Lord Kingsley. He'd proven to be most honorable, indeed.

And he had made Olivia happier than Eliza ever thought her friend could be.

"You were right not to marry Mr. Smith. And you were right about Lord Kingsley. I'll concede those two points."

"And I am right about this." Olivia still had one arm around Eliza, and she squeezed her tight. "Do you love him?"

Love.

"It makes no difference." And then she swallowed hard. "How does one know, Olivia?"

"Oh, because one thinks about him all the time. One wants to touch him at every opportunity. One cannot imagine a satisfying life without him."

Eliza thought back to all that she'd been feeling since seeing him again at the inn.

When she'd been just eight and ten, she had thought she'd loved him. She'd been more hurt by his abandonment, his rejection, than by what anyone else had said or done.

She'd not mourned the loss of Matthew nearly as much as she'd felt the loss of Henry.

But now…

She knew a different man. A mature man who'd loved and lost.

He was not all flash and charm. He did not flirt and seduce.

It was just him. And he'd established himself most firmly in her thoughts. And her dreams. More than that, she respected him, as a father, as a friend, and… as a man.

Yes, she loved him.

A knock on the door interrupted and then Lord Kingsley peered in. "I thought I'd find the two of you in here." And then he stepped inside. Eliza sat up straight and wiped at her eyes. He may be Olivia's husband, but he was also an earl.

"Crawford, Crestwood, and your brother," he told Eliza, "are departing for London in order to obtain a special license."

Eliza groaned but Olivia laughed.

"I told you," she said.

Eliza merely shook her head.

Eliza didn't sleep well that night. Why hadn't he consulted with her before racing off on such a futile errand! And to London, no less! Given, it was less than a day's ride, but as there was to be no wedding, such a journey was utterly unnecessary.

She lay in bed, alternately wondering if Olivia could possibly be right and then chastising herself at the memory of his disinclination to kiss her the other day.

He 'd also had every opportunity to kiss her when she'd

been lost in the castle corridors. She'd literally thrown herself at him.

By the time the sun crept over the horizon, she'd only slept intermittently and suspected she'd have dark circles under her eyes.

Sally entered shortly after Eliza climbed out of bed, carrying a tray of hot chocolate and biscuits.

Eliza had not drunk chocolate since she'd left school.

"Lady Kingsley said you might wish to take your breakfast in your chamber. And I'm to order a bath for you as soon as you're ready to dress." Sally was far too cheerful for Eliza's mood.

Likely Olivia was planning a ceremony already.

Eliza groaned, thinking she ought to remain in her chamber all day long—claim to be suffering from a megrim.

And then she looked out the window and sighed.

Snow!

And today was Christmas Eve! She could not remain abed. She'd promised Crawford's sisters and Charlotte and Bartholomew and Louella's oldest boy that they would collect greenery to decorate the house. She may be at sixes and sevens, but she could not break her promise. Children never forgot a broken promise.

She pressed her forehead against the window. For now, the flakes were tiny little crystals and melted as soon as they hit the ground. Hopefully, they would stay that way. She'd feel horrible if Thomas and Lord Crestwood and the duke could not make the return trip in time for the Christmas Eve festivities.

A shiver of… something… ran through her. Was it terror? Anticipation? Regret? She had no idea.

"Lady Kingsley also sent this."

Eliza turned to see the maid had returned and was holding

a scarlet dress made up of a thick velvet that matched the cape perfectly.

It was the most ridiculous, fussy, feminine, and yes, *gorgeous* garment she'd ever seen.

Leave it to Olivia.

"Well." Eliza reached out and touched the luxurious fabric. "If Lady Kingsley sent it, I might as well wear it."

* * *

IT HAD BEEN reckless of the three of them to strike out for London. It allowed for very little time for them to make the return journey in time for Christmas Eve celebrations. Henry had children to consider, as did Crawford. And Thomas Cline had an entire village of churchgoers who would expect him to deliver the Christmas sermon in barely two days' time.

Kingsley had promised to come up with something to tell Bartholomew and Charlotte though. And with Miss Cline's brother on the verge of demanding Henry meet him on a field of honor, Henry didn't want to delay.

Henry burrowed into his jacket, keeping his eyes upon the snow-covered road. They must be getting close. They'd left London hours ago.

Tucked into the inside pocket of his coat, he had a special license. He would have succeeded alone but having a duke at one's side had definitely made the undertaking less contentious.

Riding along, he half expected himself to have second thoughts, but none had come. His greatest concern was that she didn't want this as much as he did.

He'd become surprised by how much he wanted it. He hadn't wanted anything for himself in a very long time.

"Up ahead!" Crawford shouted from behind where he rode alongside his betrothed's most protective brother.

Kingsley's castle rose from behind the trees like a frozen sanctuary, less than half a mile off.

What if she'd left? Returned to Misty Brooke?

But she could not. She would wait for her brother. Of whom Henry owed a great deal. He'd protected Eliza when she needed it most.

Her brother had known Henry's actual identity. It hadn't required a great deal of asking about to discover that the man who'd ruin his sister was married. The vicar had intended to demand that Henry marry Eliza.

Of course, he'd discovered it was not possible. Thomas Cline had kept the truth from Eliza all these years. He'd known what it would do to her. Henry glanced across at the gentleman.

Apparently, the vicar hadn't been preaching out of both sides of his mouth when he'd preached all those sermon's Eliza told him about. Henry had apologized, and e and the vicar had come to a delicate détente--for now.

His mount jerked her head, as though wanting to run; she must sense they were nearing the end of their journey. Or perhaps he was the one feeling anxious.

As he turned up the snow-covered drive, sounds of laughter drifted onto the road from the surrounding forest.

And in a flash, a whirlwind in red burst through the trees. If she hadn't caught herself sharply, he would have nearly run her down.

"Henry!"

Peeking out from the white fur of her hood, Miss Cline's cheeks were flushed rosy red, and her eyes sparkled.

"Eliza." He stated the obvious.

She held one finger to her lips and ducked into a cove of hanging branches. "We're playing outside sardines, if you don't mind. And I'd appreciate not getting caught."

She certainly didn't look as though she'd spent the last thirty or so hours in deep despair.

Henry grinned and allowed his horse to continue toward the main house. He'd caused her a great deal of misery since meeting her; he'd be damned if he'd be such a bad sport as to give away her hiding place.

CHAPTER FIFTEEN

CHRISTMAS EVE

Exhausted but quite pleased with herself, Eliza followed the worn-out children up the front steps and into Kingsley's festive-looking manor.

Since she'd left earlier with all the young people, servants had hung branches of evergreen and holly over the doorway and in the windows. With the snow and the clippings and even finding the perfect tree, it had been quite impossible for Eliza to do anything other than give in to the holiday merriment.

And for some reason, when she'd seen him coming up the drive, she'd only felt joy. The men had returned safely and none of them appeared to be sporting any mortal wounds. Whatever happened would happen.

Something about this place, about the pretty dresses, the children's laughter, and being around people who had absolutely no expectations of her... It was freeing.

The butler stepped up behind her to assist her in removing her cloak but when she turned to thank him, her heart jumped. The man behind her was not the butler.

It was Henry.

She froze, her smile in place, and then all the ramifications of his presence subdued her cheerful mood.

She bit her lip.

"Do you always go running through the forest in the midst of a blizzard? At first, I thought you might be some sort of Christmas fairy." He was joking with her.

She shook her head. "We should talk."

Before Henry could respond, the actual butler stepped forward and relieved him of the fur-trimmed garment draped over his arm. Henry simply studied her quietly until they were alone again.

"I suppose. Yes. That's probably necessary." But his gaze was a tender one. "I also need to have a talk with my children." Of course, he would be concerned about them!

"They don't know anything yet." Eliza would reassure him. "Olivia asked the guests who were present in the drawing-room when Thomas… When you… Well, he requested all of them to keep it to themselves. Kingsley told Bartholomew and Charlotte that you were fetching some last-minute gifts. We all thought it best. And I agreed. Especially since…" More of her joy fled.

"Especially since?" He peered at her closely.

"Since… since it isn't real. I do wish you had not gone rushing off to London. We'll need to tell the truth. Before the children hear anything." Surely, he would agree with her—be relieved even. And yet he simply took hold of her arm and led her off into the same small parlor Olivia had taken her the day before.

Once the door closed behind him, he turned and gestured for her to sit. "And when do you suggest we inform my children of our impending marriage? After we've returned from our wedding journey?"

Oh, but why must he make this so difficult.? She did not

want to become a burden to him—a reminder of his greatest betrayal.

"But we are not betrothed," she reminded him. "It is a lie."

"The details I gave your brother." Henry was sitting beside her, close enough that she could feel the heat of his legs against hers. "The timing, I'll give you that, might have been a lie. But… I… You agreed."

Eliza covered her face with both hands and moaned. "You do not have to do this, Henry. I forgive you! I do not hate you! In fact, I've come to quite… admire your character. A person should not have to pay for one mistake for the entirety of his life! And I most certainly do not wish to become your punishment, your penance." She dropped her hands and stared at him earnestly. "I release you."

"Marrying you is not to be a penance!" The words nearly exploded from him. But then he ran a hand through his hair. "Never a punishment, Eliza. Don't you understand? Marrying you. It is the only course of action that I *can* take." His eyes pleaded with her to understand. "I *cannot allow myself* to … act upon my affections… *without* the respectability of marriage."

"But…." She was confused. "You have not kissed me. You have not wanted me now that I am… older."

"I have not kissed you, that is true. But *not* because I have not wanted to. And not because I am not attracted to you. Quite the opposite, in fact. God help me, I want *everything* with you. I want to marry you. I need to marry you. It is the only thing that I can think to do."

She blinked, still feeling confused. "Why?"

He ran his hand through his hair again, brows furrowed as though he did not know how to answer her question. "Because." He edged closer. "Because." He placed one hand along the curve of her cheek and the other on her shoulder. Leaning forward, his breath whispered along her lips.

She could not help but part them.

"How could you not know?" He spoke very near her mouth and then...

"Know what?" Her voice came out a whisper.

"Eliza," he whispered back, so close that she could taste his breath, the taste of man—the taste of only this man.

The tip of his tongue touched the soft flesh along her lips. Softly.

Gently.

Unable to stand it a second longer, she slid her fingers into his hair and pulled his head down so that his lips could claim hers completely.

And oh, oh. Yes!

His tongue thrust past her teeth, tasting, his mouth, demanding. He required no additional encouragement.

He pulled her up and against his solid frame as she twisted to be closer.

She remembered how kissing him before had been arousing, fiery and then satisfying.

But this kiss.

It was all of that but also so much more.

He'd said he wanted to marry her. She was not mistaken. He'd not gone after the special license out of some misplaced duty or honor.

He'd said he wanted her.

Eliza arched her back, her skin craving his lips, his hands, and a low groan rumbled in his chest.

"Eliza." He broke the kiss, settling his mouth on the soft skin of her cheek. He lifted one hand to return the bodice of her gown to its more modest position.

His hand trembled as he did so.

"What do I need to know? Henry?" She needed him to say it.

A shudder ran through him. "I love you." He spoke the words against her skin. "But it's not fair that I should have you. I know."

She shook her head.

How had this happened? Less than one week ago, she'd been quite comfortably settled into her position with her brother.

But no. She must be honest with herself.

She'd wanted more.

She'd wanted this.

The doorknob rattled and Eliza jerked away, smoothing her dress and skirt.

"Eliza?" Upon seeing they were presentable, Olivia pushed the door open and was followed inside by Lord Kingsley.

Henry's hand covered hers, as though he knew she might be nervous.

When she went to rise, Kingsley gestured for her to remain sitting. "Miss Cline, Crestwood." He acknowledged them both. He and Olivia took seats on the sofa across from them, appearing quite solemn. Leaning forward, resting his forearms upon his knees, the earl then stared hard at Eliza. "Your brother is anxious to proceed with a ceremony."

She squeezed Henry's hand and turned to meet his gaze. Green eyes burned back at her with purposeful intensity. And then he shifted off of the settee without releasing her hand but dropping to one knee.

Tears filled Eliza's eyes.

He loves me.

"Eliza," Henry began as though they were still alone. "I don't deserve you. God knows, I've made my share of mistakes. but I have learned from them, I believe. I will do stupid things in the future. I might forget a birthday or our anniversary, or perhaps fail to notice that you've bought a new bonnet or gown. I am only a man." He lifted that one side of his mouth, causing her heart to melt. "But my main purpose in life, from this point forward, will be to love my wife and my children, to make them happy—to protect them and keep them safe. I love you,

Eliza. Make me the happiest of men? Please? Even though I don't deserve it. Will you, Eliza? Will you marry me?"

She'd never heard of a more sincere or heartfelt proposal.

So choked up, she could hardly speak, and so she nodded. And then, nodding more emphatically, "Yes. Oh, yes, Henry!"

She didn't care that Olivia and her earl looked on. She loved him! After all these years, she never would have believed he'd come back. And then she'd never have believed they could overcome what they'd done.

She threw herself into his arms and buried her face in his neck. "I will."

She was hardly aware of Olivia's delighted laughter, nor of her brother entering the room.

But Henry managed to somehow lift them both back onto their seats and tuck her in beside him.

"Eliza." Looking considerably less riled than he had the day before, her brother stepped forward. "I need to return to Misty Brooke with all haste." He coughed into his hand, something he only did when he was feeling nervous. "But I'd be honored to preside over your nuptials."

Thomas, her dear, dear brother Thomas. She rose and crossed to him. She could never pay him back for everything he'd done for her. And he'd wanted only to protect her. She took his hands in hers and squeezed them. His eyes shone brightly, as though holding back tears. "Will you, Thomas?"

"I've the license right here, Cline," Henry spoke up behind her. "If Eliza has no objections…?"

Eliza turned to look back at Henry and smiled. "I have none."

"A wedding! A Christmas Eve wedding!" Olivia declared.

"We have clergy here. Crestwood has the license." Lord Kingsley glanced at all of them. "Olivia and I are more than happy to act as witnesses…."

"Now?" Eliza blinked. Ah, but yes, Thomas had Christmas services to hold. And they'd already waited so very long.

Henry took her hand in his. "Only if you are certain?"

She could not remember the last time she'd felt as though happiness could be in her grasp. The only objection she could think of… "We need to locate Bartholomew and Charlotte!"

And then the door opened again.

But of course, they'd been waiting outside all along, their cheeks still flushed from spending most of the morning outdoors in the cold. All smiles. And behind them, Crawford and his duchess holding their little one.

"You are going to do it then?" Bartholomew looked quite satisfied with himself.

"Surely, you didn't think we would not know?" Dear, dear Charlotte smiled at her father.

"We quite approve," Henry's son announced and his daughter nodded.

The remaining Smith children peeked in just then, followed by Lady Martha, Lady Cora, and a chagrined-looking Joseph Fellowes, accompanied by Lady Lillian.

"May we witness as well?" the duchess asked.

Thomas raised a bible in one hand and lifted a questioning brow.

"Eliza?" Henry asked. "I think it's about time, wouldn't you agree?"

"Absolutely." Eliza smiled, feeling all the magic of Christmas and so much more. "Absolutely."

EPILOGUE

THE PERFECT CHRISTMAS

None of it seemed real.

Not the gold band that shone on her left hand, nor the singing, nor the congratulations of all the other guests, nor the magnificent meal the cook at Sky Manor had prepared for the evening.

But it was. Somehow, it was.

Eliza stared at herself in the mirror. Sally had only just finished brushing out her hair and disappeared for the evening.

Olivia had moved her into a much larger chamber for this Christmas Eve night. It was adjoined with another suite, from which she could hear her husband and his valet moving about.

Henry would be joining her shortly.

She had waited so very long.

Only one week ago, she'd considered herself invisible. She leaned forward and touched her lips. Not invisible today.

No, she'd become a wife, a stepmother. She'd been a bride.

Every Christmas wish she'd ever made had come true in the matter of one afternoon.

The sounds subsided from the adjoining room and then a light knock sounded at the door.

"Come in," she beckoned and turned to face him. She wanted a good look at him, at her husband, before removing her spectacles for the evening.

The door swung open slowly. And her breath caught.

He wore an evergreen silk banyan, nearly the same color of his eyes, tied loosely at his waist. His hair had been combed, and she could tell he'd been freshly shaved.

Eliza bit her lip. It had been so long.

They'd had that one embrace in the drawing-room, before his proposal, and then a brief kiss at the end of the solemn ceremony performed by Thomas, but since then, they'd both been gushed over and congratulated and not given even two minutes to be alone in one another's company.

Suddenly, her heart raced, and she wasn't quite sure what she ought to do.

Henry closed the door behind him without removing his gaze from her.

"You are ready? I have not come too soon, have I?" He seemed only slightly hesitant.

Eliza somehow found herself rising from the vanity bench and padding across the luxurious rug so that only a few feet of space remained between the two of them.

"Not too soon." Her voice sounded hoarse. "But I'll admit to having a sudden onslaught of nerves."

He took her hand in his. "No regrets though?"

Oh, but they had so much to learn of one another. But they had a lifetime to do it. She would learn the meaning behind his expressions, and he would learn when she was sad, angry, or frustrated.

Suddenly overwhelmed with the desire to begin their lives together, she stepped even closer and placed her hands around his neck.

"None."

That one side of his mouth tilted up, making her feel warm

inside, and then the other side of his mouth tilted up as well. His smile. Oh, his smile.

And then in one swooping motion, he reached down and lifted her into his arms. "I never could have wished for a greater gift than you have already given me."

Eliza snuggled her face into his neck as he carried her to the magnificent bed.

"But I haven't given you anything." And she had nothing to give to him tomorrow.

"A second chance." His lips landed upon hers. "For happiness." He lowered her onto the mattress. "For love."

"I do love you so, Henry." She stared into his eyes. "I did when we first met, and I don't think I ever stopped."

"But you hated me—for a time," he reminded her solemnly.

Eliza touched his face. "I thought I did. But then I didn't. I understood your pain. You and I, we have both make mistakes. But if we hadn't, we would not be here now."

Henry nodded and then followed her onto the bed. "And I am so very glad to be here with you now. So grateful."

"When we met before, you said something." Eliza spoke as his mouth trailed along her jaw. "I'd forgotten it until today, when we took our vows with those that we loved all around us."

"What did I say, love?" She heard laughter in his voice, but then he drew back to stare lovingly in her eyes.

"You told me that every moment was a gift. I think you wanted to tell me the truth then. But you were lost and hurting. You said that everything could be taken away in the blink of an eye." Eliza reached up to touch the side of his face.

Henry nodded at her somberly. "We must never take such moments for granted. The joyful ones, the difficult ones, the peaceful ones."

Eliza smiled back. "Yes. We will not just take time out at Christmas to be thankful for what we have. We will try to be grateful for everyday. We will *live;* you and me, and your children.

"Our children."

"Yes."

And then he settled himself atop her. "And in this moment, Eliza," he growled as his mouth captured hers. "We will not speak of my children. In this moment, I am grateful for this." He kissed her deeply and his hands skimmed down her side. "For you."

His weight stirring sparks of delight and wanting into a glorious frenzy inside her.

"Yes, Henry," she whispered. "I think this is going to be a Perfect Christmas after all."

***

DON"T MISS Lillian's Story! **THE PERFECT ARRANGEMENT**

Dear Reader, This novella you just read, *The Perfect Christmas,* a part of the Perfect Regency Series, was originally published in *Yuletide II Happily Ever After: An Original Regency Romance Collection.* In it's original form, it did not include the prologue you read in this edition. Several readers wrote to me saying they wished I had included a scene of Eliza and Henry when they first met and when I went to release this book individually, decided it would be the perfect time to take up this challenge.

After I wrote the prologue, I felt like I came to understand Eliza and Henry better and found myself making a few changes to the original manuscript. I love these two characters, perhaps more than most, as I think forgiveness is one of the most valuable decisions we can ever make—for ourselves, but also for those who do NOT deserve it.

Thank you for reading my stories! You can find other books in this series and more by going to my website at **https://www.annabelleanders.com**

Sincerely,

Annabelle

Book 4 is next!

THE PERFECT ARRANGEMENT

THE PERFECT REGENCY SERIES

The Perfect Debutante

Louella and Cameron

The Perfect Spinster

Olivia and Gabriel

The Perfect Christmas

Eliza and Henry

The Perfect Arrangement

Lillian and Christian

ABOUT THE AUTHOR

Married to the same man for over 25 years, I am a mother to three children and two Miniature Wiener dogs.

After owning a business and experiencing considerable success, my husband and I got caught in the financial crisis and lost everything in 2008; our business, our home, even our car.

At this point, I put my B.A. in Poly Sci to use and took work as a waitress and bartender (Insert irony). Unwilling to give up on a professional life, I simultaneously went back to college and obtained a degree in EnergyManagement.

And then the energy market dropped off.

And then my dog died.

I can only be grateful for this series of unfortunate events, for, with nothing to lose and completely demoralized, I sat down and began to write the romance novels which had until then, existed only my imagination. After publishing over thirty novels now, with one having been nominated for RWA's Distinguished ™RITA Award in 2019, I am happy to tell you that I have finally found my place in life.

Thank you so much for being a part of my journey!

To find out more about my books, and also to download a free book, get all the info at my website!

www.annabelleanders.com

GET A FREE BOOK

Sign up for the news letter and download a book from Annabelle,

For **FREE**!

Sign up at **www.annabelleanders.com**

Made in the USA
Columbia, SC
10 November 2021